Fake
Me a
Match

DON'T MISS THESE OTHER GREAT BOOKS
BY LAUREN BARNHOLDT:

Rules for Secret Keeping
The Secret Identity of Devon Delaney
Devon Delaney Should Totally Know Better
Four Truths and a Lie

Fake Me a Match

LAUREN BARNHOLDT

ALADDIN MIX

New York London Toronto Sydney New Delhi

This book is a work of fiction. Any references to historical events, real people,
or real locales are used fictitiously. Other names, characters, places, and incidents are
the product of the author's imagination, and any resemblance to actual events
or locales or persons, living or dead, is entirely coincidental.

ALADDIN M!X
Simon & Schuster Children's Publishing Division
1230 Avenue of the Americas, New York, NY 10020
First Aladdin M!X edition November 2012
Copyright © 2011 by Lauren Barnholdt
All rights reserved, including the right of reproduction in whole or in part in any form.
ALADDIN is a trademark of Simon & Schuster, Inc., and related logo
is a registered trademark of Simon & Schuster, Inc.
ALADDIN M!X and related logo are registered trademarks of Simon & Schuster, Inc.
Also available in an Aladdin hardcover edition.
For information about special discounts for bulk purchases, please contact Simon & Schuster
Special Sales at 1-866-506-1949 or business@simonandschuster.com.
The Simon & Schuster Speakers Bureau can bring authors to your live event.
For more information or to book an event contact the Simon & Schuster Speakers Bureau
at 1-866-248-3049 or visit our website at www.simonspeakers.com.
Designed by Jessica Handelman
The text of this book was set in Lomba Book.
Manufactured in the United States of America 1012 OFF
2 4 6 8 10 9 7 5 3 1
The Library of Congress has cataloged the hardcover edition as follows:
Barnholdt, Lauren.
Fake me a match / by Lauren Barnholdt. — 1st Aladdin hardcover ed.
p. cm.
ISBN 978-1-4424-2258-2 (hc)
[1. Dating services—Fiction. 2. Stepsisters—Fiction. 3. Middle schools—Fiction.
4. Schools—Fiction. 5. Fund raising—Fiction. 6. Remarriage—Fiction.] I. Title.
PZ7.B2667Fak 2011
[Fic]—dc23
2011024616
ISBN 978-1-4424-2259-9 (pbk)
ISBN 978-1-4424-2260-5 (eBook)

For Aaron, always

ACKNOWLEDGMENTS

Thank you so, so much to:

Fiona Simpson, for taking over with such grace and amazingness.

Kate Angelella, for loving this book from the moment I told her the idea, and for helping to make it the best it could be.

Alyssa Eisner Henkin, for being the best agent a girl could ever ask for—I am so lucky to be working with you!

Everyone at Simon & Schuster, for working so hard on my behalf.

My mom and my sisters, for being my best friends.

Jessica Burkhart, for being the other half of Team Barnhart and an amazing friend.

Scott Neumyer and Kevin Cregg, for their support.

And Aaron, again, always, for more than I can say.

Fake Me a Match

one

SO I'M KIND OF IN THE MARKET FOR A
new best friend. Reasons:

1. My old best friend, Sophie Burns, has apparently
   decided that we are not friends anymore. I'm
   still not clear on the exact reasons for this, but
   from what I can tell, it has something to do with
   us starting seventh grade. At the beginning of
   the year she found some new, more popular
   friends (Kaci Mitchell and K.J. Reynolds), who
   love to do nothing except talk about boys, boys,
   boys. And when they're not talking about boys,
   they're texting them, following them, or getting
   their hair highlighted in order to be noticed by
   them. Don't get me wrong, I like boys as much

as the next person. (Especially Kevin Hudson, who, as far as I'm concerned, is the cutest boy at Heights Middle School, so totally cuter than Sam Humphrey, who everyone thinks is the cutest boy, but who definitely isn't due to his arrogant personality.) I just don't think they should be talked about and obsessed over all the time.

2. Everyone needs a best friend. Under normal circumstances, getting a best friend this late in the game would be almost impossible. I mean, everyone at my school either already has a best friend from elementary school, or they've already found their new middle-school best friend and ditched their old best friend for no reason (read: Sophie Burns).

Which is why it's totally lucky that I'm getting a new sister. And not a baby sister either. (Which would actually be a disaster, since who wants a baby crying and screaming and making messes all over the house?) No, I'm getting a real, honest-to-goodness thirteen-year-old stepsister. Her name is Blake (I know! How cool is that name for a girl?), and she's coming to live with us. Like, today.

"Do you think she likes green?" I ask my mom as I brush some green paint onto the wall of my room. Well, our room. Me and Blake are sharing until my mom can get all her fitness equipment cleaned out of our third bedroom. (Not like she minds. I mean, she used her treadmill maybe once, and her elliptical, like, twice. So really they're just these big dust magnets that are taking up space.)

Anyway, I decided to paint before Blake got here, and I picked this super-pretty sea-foam green that makes the whole room open up and look bright and airy. (I heard that on a home-improvement show. I know it's weird that I watch home-improvement shows. But really, they're pretty interesting. Like, did you know you can paint your refrigerator? Seriously, how cool is that? I tried to get my mom to let us paint ours red, but she was totally not having it.)

"I'm not sure," my mom says, all distracted. She's over in the corner, sitting at my desk and looking at menus for her wedding. It's in three weeks. And she *just* got engaged to Blake's dad, Will, like, two months ago. It's been totally crazy, especially for my mom, who likes to have everything done five million years ahead of time.

"What do you mean you're not sure?" I say now. I take

a step back and look at the wall. "Don't you think this color is gorgeous? It's called Sea-Foam Shell. How can that not be gorgeous?" A drip of paint slides down the wall, and I reach over and try to blot it up with the little foam brush they gave me at Home Depot. But I guess the paint must be super fast-drying or something, because it kind of just, uh, glops onto the brush. Hmmm. Well, whatever. I'm sure some touch-ups are to be expected. Even the pros can't just get it all smooth and perfect on the first try.

"No, it *is* gorgeous," my mom says. "Sorry, honey, I'm just distracted." She holds up two menus. "Do you think Italian food would be okay for a wedding? This place has an opening, but I'm not sure if Italian food is a good choice."

"I love Italian," I say. "That sounds delish." I dip my brush into the paint and start putting another coat onto the wall. This color is definitely a little darker than I thought it was going to be. But you can never really tell from a paint tag what the color is actually going to look like on the walls. Which is why you should always buy one of those little test cans. But really, who has time for one of those? I mean, Blake is going to be here TONIGHT. And I still have to make up our beds with the matching green and purple bedspreads I bought.

Ding-dong. The doorbell rings, and I scream and drop the roller I'm holding onto the floor. Sea-Foam Shell goes dribbling all over. Yikes. Good thing my mom made me put a plastic sheet down. I don't think paint comes out of carpet too well.

"Is that *them*?" I ask, panicked. "The room isn't even done yet. How can they be here *already*?"

"I don't know," my mom says. She's still looking through her glasses and down at the menus that are laid out on my desk.

"I'm a mess," I say. I look at myself in the mirror. I haven't showered yet, since I figured I'd do it after I got all messy painting. My cutoff jean shorts are splattered with bits of Sea-Foam Shell, my blond hair is a complete and total mess, and the old Villanova T-shirt of my mom's that I'm wearing has a big rip in the bottom. And I'm not sure it was there before I started painting.

"Avery," my mom says, "Will and Blake are our family now. You're going to have to get used to not freaking out whenever they show up. They're going to be living here. You don't have to get all dressed up every time they're around."

Good point. Still. Blake is from New York. As in New York *City*. I've only met her a few times, and every time she was wearing some super-fabulous outfit and doing something totally sophisticated, like ordering a cheese plate for an appetizer or something.

Oh, well. I'll just have to win her over with my personality. I rush by my mom and down the stairs, then fling open the front door.

"Hello!" I say.

"Hi," Blake says. Her long blond hair is in two French braids down the back of her head. Hmm. Maybe I should put mine like that! Then not only would we be sisters, we'd be twin sisters. Fab! Of course, we don't really look alike, but we could be fraternal.

"You guys are early," I say.

"Sorry," Will says. "We thought there would be more traffic, but the highways were totally clear."

"Good thing we brought some of our stuff," Blake says, "since the moving van won't be here until later."

Um, *some* of her stuff? I look doubtfully at the huge pile of things that are sitting on the porch behind her. And when I say pile, I literally mean pile. Clothes in big clear trash bags, a bunch of shoes that are tumbling out of a blue duffel bag, a big carton of books, a huge Ziploc bag holding a big ball of what looks like tangled-up jewelry, and a mini pink flat-screen TV with stickers stuck all over it.

"You have more stuff?" I ask.

"Yes," she says. "A lot more."

"Great!" I say brightly, even though inside I've started to freak out slightly. One, because I'm kind of a neat freak, and it doesn't seem like her stuff is, ah, very organized, and two, because our room is kind of small. But whatever. Having a sister is worth a little clutter, so yay, yay, yay! "Well, I guess we should get started bringing this stuff upstairs." I step out onto the porch and pick up a few of Blake's garbage bags. Blake picks up the smallest bag out there, the bag of shoes, and then follows me up the stairs.

Once we're in my room, she drops the bag she's holding and looks around. "You're painting," she says.

"Yeah," I tell her. "Green. I hope that's okay. It's my favorite color, and I figured it would match with whatever you have. This shade of green kind of goes with everything." Which isn't exactly true. It doesn't *really* go with her pink TV. Hmm. I wonder if you can paint TVs, too.

"It's fine," Blake says. She shrugs her shoulders. "Can I help?"

"Totally!" I say, thrilled. First day here and we're already bonding!

She picks up one of the brushes and slaps it against the wall. Green paint goes splattering into a sunburst pattern. Yikes.

"Um, don't you want to change first?" I ask her. "We have tons of old T-shirts. My mom's really into running, so every time she does a 5K or something she gets a shirt." I cross the room to my dresser and open my T-shirt drawer. "You could wear this one." I hold up a yellow shirt that we got from my school's "Run for Reading" 5K last summer.

"That's okay," she says. "I'll be careful."

Then she plops another brushful of paint right onto the wall. A blob of it goes running down and pools onto the plastic sheet that's covering the carpet. Blake doesn't seem to notice.

Hmmm. I wonder if it would be rude to go over there and tell her to be more careful. Probably. Besides, it wasn't like everything was going so perfectly before she got here. I had some blobs and runs myself. They probably make some kind of paint touch-up kit or something that we can pick up at the hardware store later. Not that I wanted to spend the morning at the hardware store, but—

"This is boring," Blake declares. She drops the paintbrush into the paint tray, and more paint splatters up and onto the wall. "Let's go see if my dad will drive us to the mall."

"Ummm . . ." I look around at my half-painted room,

and her bags that are just sitting there. "Maybe we should try to unpack a little bit first?" I'm glad she wants to hang out and everything, but how can she think of going to the mall at a time like this? We'd have to come home to a disgusting mess, which is so not the environment you want to bring new purchases into.

"Okay," Blake says, sighing like unpacking is a big imposition. She picks up one of her garbage bags and rips it down the middle. Which is kind of wasteful, when you think about it. I mean, it's a perfectly good garbage bag. She definitely could have used it again. I pick one up and open it very carefully, hoping she might learn from my example.

"Where should I put my clothes?" Blake asks.

"Oh, I cleaned out half my closet, and we brought up that dresser for you from the basement." I point to the corner where my mom put the dresser she used to use in our spare room, like, years ago.

Blake crosses the room and starts shoving her clothes into the drawers. "Done!" she declares, then slams the dresser drawer shut. Some jeans hang out over the side. "Now I just have to hang up my posters." She digs around the bottom of the ripped bag and pulls out some crumpled-up posters (all of bands I've never heard of, but that seem very indie and hip, like the kind of bands you'd know about if you lived in NYC), which she tacks up on the wall behind her bed. I want to tell her that, um, I'm going to be painting that wall at some point and so she'll just have to take them back down, but something tells me that's not the best idea.

"So you like dogs, huh?" I say, as she tacks up the last poster, the only one that's not of a band. It's of a dog, sitting in a field full of daisies and looking very cute.

"Yeah," she says. "I want to be a veterinarian when I grow up. But I'm not allowed to have one since my dad doesn't think I'm ready for the responsibility."

"Well, that's ridiculous," I say. "I'm sure you're very responsible." I try not to think about those jeans that are peeking out from the dresser and the paint splotches on the floor. She has to be responsible. I mean, she lived in New York City. She was allowed to ride the subway. By herself!

"I am," she says. "And I have a dog at my mom's house."

"You do?"

"Yeah. I really miss him."

Uh-oh. I know it's ridiculous, but I have this fear that Blake and I will become best friends and everything will be going perfectly, and then out of nowhere she'll somehow decide that she wants to go and live with her mom in Virginia. I know, it's crazy, right? But when you've already had one best friend ditch you out of nowhere, a person can start to get a little paranoid.

"You know," I say, suddenly getting a brilliant idea, "I bet my mom would be able to convince your dad to let us have a dog."

"You think?" Blake tilts her head and bites her lip, and I move over and sit down next to her on her bed.

"Yeah," I say. "My mom's actually pretty laid-back when it comes to things like that." I've always been a good kid, which means that when I want something, my mom usually trusts me to know that I can handle it. Which is really good when it comes to certain things, like this. Although . . . I'm not sure I really *want* a dog. I mean, I like animals and everything, but dogs shed, and they make messes, and they need to be walked, like, all the time. Maybe we could get a small dog, though. I've heard those are easier to exercise.

"I want a huge dog," Blake says. Okay, then. "A black one."

"Um . . . well, it will probably depend on—"

"So should we go ask her?"

"Right *now*?"

"Yeah."

"Um . . ." I think about it. I mean, there's no real reason not to, right? No time like the present and all that. "Sure."

We head downstairs to where my mom and Will are making lunch in the kitchen. Blake's shoe must have gotten a tiny little bit of wet paint on it, because as she walks, little bits of gummy paint get deposited onto the carpet. I really hope I have a chance to get to the hardware store.

two

SO IF YOU WANT TO KNOW THE TRUTH about how I feel about my mom getting married to Will, I think it's pretty great. And I'm not just saying that because it's what I think I'm supposed to say. My parents have been divorced since I was a baby, and my dad has never been around. So I don't even remember what it was like for my parents to be together, and I'm really glad my mom's going to finally have someone around to do things with. (And to kill spiders for her, since my mom is terrified of them. And mice, too. One time a mouse climbed into our washing machine without anyone knowing and got, like, washed with the clothes. It made her really hysterical, and I had to reach in and get it out. Which wasn't that big of a deal. I just put gloves on and tossed it into the woods behind our house.)

Anyway, I don't think my mom *needs* to have a man around to do that stuff, but it's nice that she has someone to watch movies with and talk about books with and just . . . you know, *be* with. Will is her best friend. And that makes me really happy.

But as I'm falling asleep that night, I start to think that Blake doesn't feel the same way. Maybe it has to do with the fact that her mom and dad just got divorced a couple of years ago, or maybe it has to do with the fact that she had to move from New York City to our small town in Massachusetts. I mean, she hasn't done anything *specific* to make me think she might not be so into this whole my-mom-marrying-her-dad-thing. But she *has* been a little weird. Like with the "let's get a dog" situation. She was all quiet when I asked my mom if we could get one, she was all quiet when my mom said yes, and she was all quiet when we went online and looked up a local animal shelter and made an appointment to go down there after school tomorrow.

I kind of wanted to talk to her about it, but I didn't want her first night at our house to be awkward, so I chalked it up to her just being in a new place and being nervous. And by the time we were ready for bed, she'd definitely mellowed out.

So I fall asleep without bringing it up, and when we

wake up the next morning, Blake's in a super-chipper mood. She's practically singing as we get ready (which is nice, even if she did take a thirty-minute shower, leaving me with, like, no hot water).

"So what's the cafeteria like?" she asks as we wait for the bus. She keeps looking down the street, like she's afraid she's going to miss it. She's never ridden the bus to school before, which is kind of funny. Although I guess she probably thinks it's pretty funny that I'm afraid to take the subway by myself.

"Um, I guess it's just a standard cafeteria," I say. "You know, hot lunch line, that sort of thing." Not that I have to worry about the hot lunch line. I have the same lunch every single day. A ham and cheese sandwich, an apple, Doritos, and two Oreo cookies. I rotate my drink between my fave three juices: apple, grape, and pineapple.

"No, I mean, where does everyone sit? Like, who are the popular girls?" She reaches into her Coach purse, pulls out a small tube of lip gloss, and lines her lips.

"The popular girls?" I ask warily. Blake isn't supposed to be worried about the popular girls. She's supposed to be *my* best friend. I decide to sidestep the question. "Well, if you want to get to meet some people, maybe you should stay after with me today for student council."

"Student council?" She wrinkles up her tiny little nose and looks confused, like the thought of the popular girls being on student council makes no sense. Which it kind of doesn't, since the popular girls aren't really on student council. They mostly play sports—soccer, lacrosse, and track are where Sophie Burns and Kaci Mitchell and K.J. Reynolds can be found. And those three are the most popular girls in the school. Not that the kids on student council are dorky or anything. They're just popular in a different way.

The bus comes rumbling around the corner then, and I mount the stairs and head for my usual seat—middle of the bus, right-hand side. But for some reason, Blake keeps walking right by me and toward the back.

"Come on," she says. "Let's sit back here."

"Um," I say. "Well . . . uh, I always sit here." The back of the bus is not somewhere you can just *decide* to go. You, like, have to be invited or something. Actually, that's not even true. You can't even be invited. You just have to somehow start sitting there at the beginning of the year. At the beginning of your life, even. And if you don't, you can't just decide you're going to start. That's so not how it works.

"Why?" Blake asks. "Are there assigned seats?"

"Well, no . . ."

"Then come on."

I sigh, then follow her to the back of the bus, where Blake plops herself down in the second-to-last seat. She probably would have been crazy enough to have sat in the last seat, except it's already occupied. By two boys. Sam Humphrey and Hayden Frye.

"Hey, Avery," Sam says. He pops his head over the seat and looks at me. "Who's your friend?"

Sam's in our grade, super popular, and plays on the JV lacrosse team. Which is like a huge deal, to be in seventh grade and play JV. That's, like, the high school team. People think he might be the next LeBron James or whatever the equivalent lacrosse star is. Not that I've ever seen Sam play. I don't go to many lacrosse games. Although maybe I should start. School spirit and all that. Anyway, the only reason he knows my name is because we're on student council together.

"Um, this is my . . ." Sister? Friend? Roommate?

"I'm Blake," Blake says, before I can figure out how to introduce her. "Who are you?"

Sam grins, like he can't possibly imagine anyone not knowing who he is. "I'm Sam," he says. "And you're cute."

He sits back down in his seat, which is a good thing, because my mouth, like, drops open. I'm so shocked that

I drop my homework planner onto the floor of the bus.

"So I guess I'm supposed to go to the main office," Blake says as I retrieve the planner and try to brush some of the dirt off the pages. Gross. "To get my schedule and stuff. Ugh, starting a new school really sucks."

"Um, hello," I say. "Did you not just hear Sam Humphrey call you cute?"

"I know," she says, all giggly-like. "I think he's cute too. I just love guys with floppy hair, don't you?"

"I guess so," I say. The thing is, I don't know if I like guys with floppy hair. I think I prefer their hair spiky. But that's because the only guy that I would even think about liking is Kevin Hudson, and he has spiky hair. But I don't like him because of his hair. I like him because he's very smart and always lets me play his DS whenever the teachers aren't looking.

And then, without even announcing it or anything, Blake stands up, reaches behind us, and takes off Sam Humphrey's hat. Like, right off his head. And puts it on her own. She is wearing Sam Humphrey's hat! Like it's nothing! On her first day—no, her first *five minutes* at our school!

"Hey," Sam says. "Give it back!" But he says it more in an "If you don't give it back I'm going to take it and I'll like it" kind of way, not like he's really mad.

"Come and get it," Blake says. She grins, showing off her perfect smile that's never going to need braces.

"Fine," Sam says.

And that's how I end up squooshed up against the bus window, with Blake in the middle and Sam on the outside, while they talk and flirt the whole way to school.

Whatever. I mean, it's not like I wanted her to come to school and be a total outcast. That's so not nice. But I thought she'd need me at least a *little* bit. You know, to show her around, to let her know where her classes are, to point out the girls to avoid, to tell her who the nicest teachers are. But I didn't even get a chance to do any of that stuff.

The morning, a breakdown:

> Before Homeroom: I walk Blake to the office and am then sent to class by Mr. Fierra, our guidance counselor. Which I think is so totally unfair, since I should be the one to be able to show Blake around. I'm going to be her sister, for God's sake! I try to tell him that, but he won't have it. He just sends me off to class and says I can find her later.

Homeroom: I meet Blake at her locker
(which I only know the location of since I
stole a look at the paper Mr. Fierra was
holding when he was unfairly and rudely
sending me back to class), and walk her
to first period. But once we get there, I
don't even have a chance to tell her the
girls to look out for before going to my
own class, because Sophie Burns jumps
out of her seat and yells, "Hey, new girl,
come sit here!" like, right away. And
Blake does!

First Period: I don't see her at all.

Second Period: I don't see her at all.

Third Period: I don't see her at all,
but Sam Humphrey asks me if Blake
is going to be taking advanced math.
Which I realize I have no idea about,
so I just give him this super-vague
answer like, "Wouldn't you like to know?"
because I don't want to admit that I
don't know. Also, how annoying is it that

Sam Humphrey is in advanced math? It
doesn't really seem fair, especially since
I wanted to be in advanced math, but
I missed the cutoff by, like, two points.
(I wanted to be able to look at the
Scantron sheet to double-check it, but the
advanced math teacher, Mrs. Milhomme,
said it wasn't allowed, which is kind of
ridiculous if you ask me, since with most
things, you can definitely get a recount.
Even presidential elections.)

Fourth Period: I don't see Blake at all.

By the time lunch rolls around, I'm feeling slightly
out of sorts, so I grab my lunch from my locker and take
my seat at my usual table, with Rina Nichols and Jess
Lukey. Rina and Jess are my friends from student council, and they've been BFF since, like, forever. They're nice
enough, but you can't penetrate them, you know? Like,
you're always going to be the third wheel. It's like being
on one of those reality shows where someone's going to
get voted off, and you know you're always going to be the
one to go. The other thing about Rina and Jess is that
they have this annoying habit of referring to each other

as "bestie buddies," which I just cannot get behind. Call her your BFF like everyone else.

"Where's your new sister?" Rina asks.

"Yeah, is she going to sit with us? I can't wait to meet her." Jess takes a bite of her corn salad and looks at me expectantly. She's eating from one of those bento box things. I wonder if I should get into those. They seem super healthy.

"I don't know where she is," I say honestly. I pull my phone out of my bag and send Blake a quick text. I've been holding off on doing that all morning, because I didn't want to seem like a psycho stalker. But now that it's lunchtime, I think a text is definitely allowed. WHERE R U? I hit send, then open up one of my Oreo cookies and lick out the frosting. Yum. My phone vibrates, and I reach down and look at it. WHO IS THIS? Okay, so apparently when we exchanged numbers in an email last month, Blake didn't take the time to program me into her phone.

AVERY! SAVING U SEAT NEAR DOOR IN CAF XX

The reply comes fast. SITTING WITH SOPHIE—LOOK UP!

Oh, for the love of . . . I look up. And there she is, over in the corner, waving at me. "Come sit!" she mouths.

Obviously she doesn't know that Sophie and I are so not friends. So I just smile at her, and shrug, and pretend I can't hear her, and go back to my food, even though my heart feels heavy, like a stone sinking to the bottom of the ocean.

"Why is your sister sitting with Sophie Burns?" Rina wants to know.

"I have no idea."

"Well, are they friends?"

"I'm not sure," I say honestly. "They just met today."

Rina and Jess don't say anything. They know my history with Sophie, and they know better than to bring it up. "Well, maybe she wants to come to the student council meeting," Jess says. "We need more people for the school charity project that's coming up."

"Good idea," I say, forcing a smile on my face. I'm sure I could convince Blake to stay after for student council. Cheered, I eat the rest of my Oreos.

But after school, when I find Blake outside and try to get her to stay after for the student council meeting, she says, "That's okay, Avery. I don't think I'm the student-council type." And then she hops on to our bus and flounces all the way to the back.

So by the time I get to the quad (we have our meetings outside when it's warm enough, since our faculty adviser, Ms. Tosh, thinks it inspires creativity), I'm not in that great of a mood.

I sit down on the ground next to Rina and Jess, after making sure I spread my jacket out. Grass stains are a total pain in the butt to get out of clothes. Even when you use a stain stick.

"Hey," they say in unison.

"Hi," I say, trying not to be annoyed at the fact that they're speaking in unison, and my soon-to-be stepsister who was supposed to be my soon-to-be BFF is hanging out with Sophie Burns and flouncing to the back of the bus without me.

"Hey," Kevin Hudson says. He's sitting on the grass next to me. He gives me a little wave, and when he does, his arm brushes against mine, and I feel my heart get a little sparkly. That's what I call it when a boy makes me get all weird. It's like sparks that start in your heart and end up in your stomach and your brain and everywhere else.

"Is everyone here?" Ms. Tosh is asking. She's super young and funny, but she's also strict at the same time. You can't get away with anything in her class, but she makes things interesting, and she's fair.

"Yes," we chorus.

"Okay, so today we're going to be talking about the annual student council charity project," she says. I sit up straight and shoot a look at Kevin. We've been talking about the school charity project for, like, ever. It's kind of a big deal.

"Already?" he whispers to me. "I thought that wasn't going to be until next month."

"I heard they had to move it up because of the new middle school," Rina says. They're building a new middle school in our district, but it's not going to be ready until halfway through the year, and when it is, they're going to move us all over. I guess they figured that with all the confusion, it would be too much to have a charity project going on at the same time. I'm all for moving it up, since I'm a pretty impatient person, and I've been waiting for this for, like, all my life. Well. At least for the past two years, ever since the girl who was running it then came to our front door selling raffle tickets and I thought she was cool.

"Now, as your faculty adviser, I need to pick someone to be in charge of the project," she says. She's looking down at her notebook.

"I'll do it," Sam Humphrey says, without even raising his hand. I resist the urge to roll my eyes. I should have told Blake that Sam was in student council. She definitely would have signed up then. But I wanted her to sign up because she wanted to spend time with me, not because she wanted to flit around, grabbing Sam Humphrey's hat

♥ 25 ♥

and flirting during student council. Which would have been very inappropriate.

"Thank you, Sam," Ms. Tosh says. "But I've already picked the person who I'm going to be putting in charge. And that person is Avery LaDuke."

"Me?" I squeak. I'm thrilled, of course. I mean, this is a huge honor! Seventh graders never get to run the charity project.

"Yes," Ms. Tosh says, smiling. "Meet me before school tomorrow and we'll go over all the particulars." She pushes her totally trendy wire spectacles up on her nose and looks at Sam. "Sam can be your assistant."

"Cool with me," Sam says, shooting me a smile. "Congratulations, Avery."

"Thanks," I say.

Rina reaches over and squeezes my hand, and Kevin leans in and whispers, "Way to go, Avery."

My face is flushed with excitement, and my supersparkly feeling lasts the rest of the meeting and the whole late bus ride home.

three

"I JUST . . . I GUESS I JUST DON'T REALLY like any of them," Blake is saying. It's later that afternoon, and we're standing in this really long hallway at the animal shelter, surrounded by cages and cages of dogs. Black dogs, brown dogs, spotted dogs, old dogs, young dogs, fluffy dogs, scruffy dogs . . . you name it, they're here. It's actually kind of depressing. Which is maybe why my mom and Will didn't want to come back here. My mom doesn't do so good with depressing. So they filled out the application and paid the adoption fee, and then they went next door to buy new backpacks at L.L. Bean—they're going hiking in the Berkshires for their honeymoon—and left me and Blake to pick out the pup.

"You don't like any of the dogs?" the shelter worker

asks. She's this semi-snotty high school girl named Mia who's wearing the brightest pink lipstick I've ever seen. She definitely doesn't seem like the type to be interested in animals, but I guess you can't judge a book by its cover. Or its lipstick, haha. "That's a first. Usually peeps want to take them all home."

"Yeah, well, I don't know, they just . . . I don't see myself as the owner of any of them." Blake shrugs, obviously not disturbed by her lack of interest in the dogs or the fact that the shelter worker just used the word "peeps."

"You don't see yourself as the owner of any of them?" I ask. "But you love dogs!"

"You just need to play with one of them, honey," Mia says. As she talks, the overhead light flashes off the silver stud of her tongue piercing. "I'll get you out some nice doggies, and we'll bring them back to the play area, and you can bond with one of them, okay? There's nothing to be afraid of." Her tone is really condescending, and she sounds like she's about one step away from patting Blake on the head.

"She's not afraid of dogs," I assure her. "She loves dogs! You love dogs, don't you, Blake?" She loved them last night, anyway, when she was ruining my new paint job by putting up her stupid dog poster. Her notebooks and binders even have stickers of puppies all over them, interspersed with pictures of the NYC skyline and designer clothes.

"I guess," Blake says. "I mean, I did love dogs."

"We'll take that one," I say, pointing to a medium-size cream-colored dog sitting in his cage, mostly because his tail is wagging so fast I'm afraid if we don't take him out, it's going to fall off. "And that one." I point to a black one that's just lying there, looking around kind of regally. "We'll play with those two, please."

"Wonderful!" Mia says. She's still being condescending, but I forgive her since I have bigger problems on my hands, i.e., that we're at a dog shelter and Blake has obviously forgotten and/or lost her desire for a dog.

"Come on." I take Blake's hand and lead her into the little room where you play with the dogs. It has white walls, with a built-in bench that runs all around the perimeter, and a sign outside that says DOGGIE PLAY AREA. You'd think they could have come up with something a little more original than "Doggie Play Area." I push through the little swinging doors and sit down on the bench, pulling Blake with me. "What is *wrong* with you?" I demand.

"What do you mean?" She has her phone out, and she's texting away to God knows who.

"What do I mean? You begged and begged me to bring you here and get you a dog!"

"No, I didn't," she says. She shrugs, her fingers flying over the keyboard.

I stare at her in shock. "Yes, you did," I say. "Remember? I said, 'Maybe my mom would let us have a dog,' and then *you* said, 'Let's ask her now, oh please, oh please, oh please,' and then *I* said—"

"Here we are!" Mia sings. She pushes through the door, and the dogs come running into the room. Wow. They're a little . . . wilder than I'd thought they'd be. I've never had a dog before. Actually, I've never had any kind of pet, unless you count the fish I won at a fair when I was five. Which I don't think you do, since it was only alive for three weeks. Which is actually quite long when it comes to fish.

The gold-colored dog jumps up on me and starts licking my face, and the black one jumps up and curls up in Blake's lap.

"How cute!" Mia says, smiling. "They like you guys! You have a very hard decision to make!"

"Yes, um, well . . ." The golden retriever is now pulling at the bottom of my pant leg, jumping around all playfully. He better not rip these jeans. They're my favorite pair, perfectly worn in from lots of wearing and lots of washing and lots of . . . oh, ew. He's a slobberer, this one. "We should probably be left alone," I say to Mia pointedly. "You know, so we can talk about things."

"Oh, of course," Mia says. But her tone is all annoyed, and she has a tight smile on her face. As soon as she closes the door behind her, I turn to Blake. She's sitting there calmly, stroking the back of the little black dog, still looking at whatever texts she's getting.

"So which one do you think?" I ask brightly. The golden retriever has abandoned my jeans and is sniffing all around the room. Then he comes over and starts sniffing around in my backpack, which I've set down over by the door. "Hey," I say. "Stay away from that."

But he doesn't listen. He reaches in and pulls out a piece of paper, and starts batting it around the floor happily. Good thing it's blank. I don't think my teachers are really going to believe the whole dog-ate-my-homework thing.

"I definitely think the black one," I tell Blake, who's still just sitting there, petting the dog in her lap and not saying anything. "That dog seems very calm and relaxed." I walk over and sit down next to Blake, giving the dog a little pat on the head. "Aren't you, pooch?" The dog stares at me, bored.

Blake stands up and sets the dog gently on the

ground. "It's up to you, Avery," she says, shrugging. "You should pick whichever one you want." And then she goes marching out of the room.

We end up with both of them. I know. Two dogs. It's completely crazy, since:

1. I never even wanted a dog in the first place,
2. now Blake apparently doesn't want a dog either, and
3. the golden retriever is nuts.

But my mom and Will thought it was important that Blake and I each have our own dogs, since it turns out they'd read some kind of ridiculous article online about how when you're blending families, it's important for each person to keep their own identity and not feel like they have to conform to the other family's rules. Which doesn't make sense, since by getting a dog in the first place we're already conforming to the other family's rules, since Blake had already been told she couldn't have a dog!

But when I pointed that out, my mom didn't want to hear it. I know, because she said, "Avery, I don't want to hear it." And so then Mia told them that the golden

retriever had taken a shine to me, and the black one—
which I guess is some kind of a dachshund mix—had
taken a shine to Blake. Which was ridiculous, since neither one of them had really taken a shine to anyone.
(Those were Mia's words, by the way, not mine. I don't
say things like "take a shine.")

And then my mom told Mia that we'd be taking both,
and then Mia told her that it was a two-hundred-and-
fifty-dollar extra adoption fee, and then Will pulled out
his credit card and now we have two dogs!

Which is how Blake and I end up walking the two
of them that night, outside around our neighborhood,
right after dinner when we should be inside, working
on our homework or trading makeup tips or watching
reality TV or whatever it is that soon-to-be stepsister
BFFs do.

"I don't know why I got stuck with the one that mis-
behaves," I say, as the dog at the end of my leash stops
and just starts looking around the street, as if he's confused. Which I guess he probably is. I mean, he has no
idea what's going on. He doesn't even know he's a dog,
I don't think. He thinks he's human, which is proven by
the fact that he sat in my lap the whole ride home.

Blake doesn't say anything. She just keeps walking.
Her dog, of course, is like the most perfect dog ever.

Seriously, she could be on Animal Planet or something. She just walks along, all prancy-like. She's even dodging the mud puddles, stepping over them delicately with her paws.

"I'm naming my dog Gus," I announce. "What are you naming yours?"

"I don't know," Blake says, and then shrugs.

"All right," I say, stopping in the middle of the street. Gus pulls on the end of the leash, but I ignore him. "What the heck is going on with you? You begged and begged for a dog, and now you don't even care that we have one! Two of them, even!"

"I didn't beg and beg for a dog," Blake says, rolling her blue eyes like she can't believe how dramatic I'm being.

My mouth drops open. But then I realize that she's right. I mean, she didn't *really* beg and beg. She just kind of mentioned that she was into dogs, and that her dad wouldn't let her have one, and then I had to open my big mouth and say I would talk to my mom. But still. She *wanted* a dog. She has dogs all over her binder and now all over our room. Which is a mess, by the way. There are still half-painted walls, and some of it's all smudgy. But who's had time to fix it with all the time we've spent hanging out in animal shelters? Not to mention the fact that my mom's not going to be too thrilled about having to shell out more money for paint supplies when she just spent five hundred dollars on dogs.

"Yeah, but you—"

"So what's the deal with Sam?" Blake asks suddenly.

"What?" Gus pulls on the leash, and I jerk forward a little, struggling to keep my balance.

"Sam, you know, from the bus?"

"Sam Humphrey?"

"Yeah."

"What do you mean, what's his deal?"

She sighs and pushes her hair out of her face. The front part is all wavy from the braid she had it in earlier. "I mean, what's his deal? Does he have a girlfriend?"

"Sam?" I laugh. "No, he doesn't have a girlfriend." Gus pulls on the leash some more, and I pick up the pace to try and keep up.

"Why's that funny?" she wants to know. "He's cute."

"Yeah, he's just . . . he's a flirt," I say. "He flirts with everyone."

"Oh." But Blake doesn't look disappointed. She just looks determined.

"Do you like him?" I ask nonchalantly, even though the answer is obvious. Of course she likes him. But I need to hear it from her. That's what sisters do, right? Tell secrets.

"I don't know him well enough to like him," she says. "But he's supercute. And nice. And funny. And smart."

Wow. For someone who doesn't know him well enough to like him, she's obviously already formed an opinion. And I would not describe Sam Humphrey as nice. Or funny. Maybe kind of smart. If I had to pick one word to describe him, I would call him cocky. And annoying.

"Your dog is digging," Blake says.

I look down and see Gus happily pawing at some red and gold flowers one of our neighbors has planted around their mailbox. Crap, crap, crap. "No," I say. "Bad dog." I try to make my voice sound authoritative, like I've seen the Dog Whisperer do. Actually, I'm not sure that the Dog Whisperer does that. I think he just ignores dogs or something? Or shows them who their pack leader is? Am I Gus's pack leader? "Stop!" I say. "I am your pack leader and I command you to stop immediately!"

But Gus doesn't listen. He just keeps digging away.

"You really need to give that dog a name," Blake says. "Otherwise how is he going to know you're talking to him?"

"I told you," I say. "I named him Gus." I turn back to the dog. "Gus!" I say. "Gus, stop it!" I give his leash a tug, but Gus is too strong. Plus obviously he's not going to respond to his name, since this is the first time anyone's ever called him that. I wonder what his old name was. Mia really should have provided us with that information. I don't think she was too good at her job. We probably should have filled out a comment card.

The front door of the house Gus is destroying bangs open. Great. Just great. Now I have to get ready to charm some adults and come up with a whole story to tell whoever comes out about how Gus is a troubled dog from a shelter with a bad past. He doesn't really have a bad past. He just had to be given up when his family had a kid who was allergic. Which I guess actually *is* a bad past, just being abandoned by your family. I mean, he's obviously very troubled, and I, out of the kindness of my heart, have taken him into my family, even though I have my plate full with school and the student council charity project and a new soon-to-be stepsister BFF and painting my room and my mom's wedding and—

Oh, God. It's not an adult coming out of the house. It's a boy. A boy with floppy hair and a green T-shirt. A boy who is Sam Humphrey.

Okay, so it turns out that Blake is quite the flirt. Like, *quite* the flirt. I mean, I saw her this morning on the bus and everything, but that was nothing compared to the skills that she's displaying now. I had no idea just how talented she was.

Although now that I think about it, I do remember this one time when we were at her apartment in NYC and we all ordered pizza and Blake went to the door and ended up standing there talking to the teenage delivery guy for, like, way longer than was necessary. At the time I just thought she was having trouble figuring out the tip.

"Sooo," she says to Sam. She twirls her hair around her finger and smiles. "That would be great if you could help me with my dog. I bet you're an *ahh-mmazing* dog trainer."

I try to resist the urge to roll my eyes, but then I do it anyway. I guess Sam is really good with dogs. At least, that's what he's been telling us, but I'll believe it when I see it. You can't really take his word on anything. Last year our sixth-grade class set up this bake sale to raise money for our field trip to Six Flags, and Sam claimed he was this world-class baker and was going to make these amazing cookies and make tons of money and blah blah blah. He showed up with a pan of burnt brownies.

"Yeah, totally," Sam says. "We should get together tomorrow after school." Apparently Sam's grandparents live in the house where Gus decided to relandscape the lawn. So even though Sam only lives a few streets over and rides our bus, when he's visiting his grandma he's only a few *houses* down. Which definitely cannot be good for Blake's crush. I mean, she's obviously very . . . aggressive. What if she starts going over to his grandparents' house all the time, just showing up without warning? I don't think that would be very good. They might call the police on her or something.

"That sounds great," I say. "Tomorrow, after school, Blake can come over and you can help her train . . ." I trail off, since Blake's dog doesn't have a name.

"Princess," Blake supplies.

"Princess?" I ask incredulously. Princess? Talk about a lame name for a dog.

"Yeah," Blake says.

"It fits," Sam says. He kneels down and pats Princess, who seems to like her new name. She wags her tail politely and then sits down primly on the sidewalk. Gus, on the other hand, seeing that someone else is getting attention, rushes over and starts licking Sam's face. Yuck. "Since her owner is such a princess."

"A princess who hasn't found her prince," Blake says. Oh. My. God. I might vomit soon.

"Time to go!" I say. "I think I hear my mom calling us in for dinner."

"Wait," Blake says as I pull on her arm. "Did you say you're on student council?"

"Yeah," Sam says.

"Well, Avery was telling me all about it, and it sounds fascinating."

"It does?" Sam asks.

"It does?" I ask. Student council is a lot of things, but fascinating is definitely not one of them. And I wasn't telling her all about it. All I said was that she should stay after for the meeting. Which she didn't do.

"Totally," Blake says. More hair twirling.

"Cool," Sam says. "We're having a meeting tomorrow morning, before school. In the small cafeteria. You should come."

"Definitely!" Blake says.

I sigh. Sam goes inside, and Gus pulls us home.

The next morning, at 8:00 a.m., Will drops us off in front of school.

"Have fun, girls!" he says.

"Bye," I say, waving at him through bleary eyes. I'm feeling a little bit grumpy, since Blake took, like, five million hours in the bathroom this morning, when I had to get in to take a shower. So we're running late, and I didn't even have time to eat breakfast. Everyone knows that going to school without having breakfast is, like, the number one wrong thing to do. It sets you up to have a totally bad day.

"Here," Blake says as we walk up the cobblestones toward the door by the caf. "I snagged you a Pop-Tart."

"Thanks," I say gratefully. Processed wheat with a smear of fake sugar in the middle is definitely not what the government had in mind when they said to start your day off with a good breakfast, but whatevs. I'm hungry, and I love Pop-Tarts. And this one even has frosting.

When we get inside, we sit down with Rina and Jess.

"This is Blake," I say. I still don't really know how to introduce her. I mean, she's not really my sister. She's not even my *step*sister yet. She's not my friend. Yet. So what is she? My soon-to-be stepsister? "And this is Rina and Jess."

"Hi," Blake says. She smiles, but her eyes are already moving around the room, looking for Sam. "Where does Sam usually sit?"

"Sam Humphrey?" Rina asks. She wrinkles up her nose. "He usually sits in the back."

"Come on, Avery," Blake says. "Let's go sit in the back." She takes my hand and starts to pull me up from my seat. The side of her bangle bracelet cuts into my thumb, and I pull my hand back.

"No," I say. "I always sit up here with Rina and Jess. Plus, um, today we're finding out what the student council charity project is going to be, and so I need to sit up here."

"Avery got chosen to lead the whole thing," Rina says.

"It's a totally amazing accomplishment," Jess agrees. "They never, ever pick a seventh grader."

"Well, it's not *that* big of a deal," I say, feeling my face get hot. "I mean, they *did* pick a seventh grader a few years ago, Mitchell Huntsman, he—"

"Hey!" Sam Humphrey says, cutting me off as he plops down next to us.

"Oh," Blake says, apparently thrown. "I thought you always sat in the back."

"I did," Sam says. "Until I saw you sitting in the front."

Rina and Jess look at each other, their eyebrows raised. But before anyone can say anything—or worse, before Blake can start flirting back—Ms. Tosh is calling the meeting to order.

"Thanks for getting here so early, guys," she says. "It's really important that we do a good job on our charity project this year, since all the money is going to Children's Hospital Boston."

Wow. That's a very good charity. It's going to look super fab on my college applications. I can see it now.

*In seventh grade, I helped to raise x number of dollars for
Children's Hospital Boston, all by taking the lead on our
student council charity project.*

"Now, as for the fund-raiser itself," she says. "We're
going to be doing something very exciting this year."

The anticipation is totally killing me. I see Rina and
Jess smile at me, and my heart flies up to my throat. I
glance over at Blake, but she's writing notes back and
forth with Sam. Ugh.

"This year," Ms. Tosh says, "we are going to be doing
a student council matchmaking service!"

She beams. I frown, shaking my head. Surely I've
misheard her.

"What did she say?" I whisper to Rina.

"She said it's going to be a matchmaking service!"
Rina sounds just as excited as Ms. Tosh.

My hand shoots up into the air before I can stop
it. "Excuse me," I say. "I thought you just said we were
going to be doing a matchmaking service, but that
cannot be right." Is it possible she means, like, career
matchmaking? You know, where you take one of those
aptitude tests and they tell you what career you're
suited for?

"Oh, it's right," Ms. Tosh says. "You see, we polled the
students on what kind of charity project they'd like to

see this year, and a matchmaking service was at the top of the list."

"What poll?" I ask. "I don't remember any poll." And if there had been a poll, I definitely would not have voted for a *matchmaking* service. How the heck am I going to put that on my college applications? *As a seventh grader, I raised money for Children's Hospital Boston by running a matchmaking service?* Forget about Harvard, I'll get laughed right out of Framingham State.

"You remember," Sam chimes in helpfully. "The poll? I ran it with Hayden Frye, we sat outside the cafeteria and asked people?"

I rack my brain and come up with a vague memory of Sam and his friend Hayden sitting outside the big cafeteria with a clipboard and a blue Sharpie, marking down some such nonsense.

"That was a poll?" I screech. "I thought you guys were just being annoying."

"Yes," Ms. Tosh says. "Sam and Hayden did an excellent job. They're actually the ones who came up with the idea of the matchmaking service in the first place."

"If they came up with the idea, then how could it be that the students wanted it?" I shoot Sam a suspicious look. This poll is starting to sound shadier by the second. Like dirty politics.

"If the kids couldn't come up with something, we suggested a matchmaking service," Sam says. "You'd be surprised how many people were totally into it."

Actually, no I wouldn't. Not when he puts it that way. When he puts it that way, with him standing outside the cafeteria, accosting girls and making them lose their mental faculties, then asking them if they want a matchmaking service, of course the overall majority are going to say yes! They were being influenced by his dimples and his floppy hair and his perfect smile.

"Ms. Tosh," I try. "No disrespect to Sam and Hayden"—I take a moment here to flash a smile at both of them—"but this poll doesn't sound all that scientific. And without really knowing if it's what the students want, I move that we do another poll, and/or brainstorm other ideas. How about those Livestrong bracelets we sold last year?"

"Those bracelets only made us about a hundred dollars," Sam says cheerfully. "The project was kind of a failure."

"I think a matchmaking service sounds amazing," Blake says. I want to remind her that she also thought a dog sounded amazing, and once it (they) got there, she changed her mind real quick.

"We're doing a matchmaking service," Ms. Tosh says. "Now are there any other questions?"

Whatever. Teachers are rational people, right? I mean, they have to be to deal with a bunch of thirteen-year-olds all day. They need to be able to teach us how to make the right decisions, and how to reason things through logically. I mean, they have to be rational people on *some* level. At least, that's what I'm counting on after the meeting, when I approach Ms. Tosh, hoping I can talk some sense into her.

"Hey, Avery," she says. She's gathering up her papers and folders from the table and sliding them into her leather briefcase. "How are you doing? Are you feeling overwhelmed? I know there was a lot to take in there, but we're going to get through it, and of course I'll be here for you every step of the way. You're going to do a fantastic job."

"I'm not overwhelmed," I say. I don't get overwhelmed. "I just wanted to talk. About the matchmaking service. I mean, it's kind of . . . I don't want to sound snobby, but it's kind of silly, isn't it?" I give her the smile I use on adults sometime, the smile that tells them that I'm way mature for my age, and that they should listen to me because I'm an old soul and know what I'm talking about.

"Silly? How so?"

"Um, well." I shift my weight back and forth on my sneakers nervously. "I just mean that it doesn't really . . . I mean, it just looks kind of weird to raise money for a charity by doing matchmaking, doesn't it?" I force a laugh, but Ms. Tosh doesn't laugh back. She doesn't even smile. God, I really should have planned this out better.

"Have you ever heard of Mark Zuckerberg, Avery?" Ms. Tosh asks. She picks up the silver tumbler that's sitting on the table in front of her and takes a sip of her coffee.

"Of course," I say. "He's the guy who founded Facebook."

"That's right," she says. "And did you know that Mr. Zuckerberg donated one hundred million dollars to the Newark, New Jersey, school system?"

"Um, no," I say. "But I don't know what that has to—"

"And do you think that the Newark, New Jersey, school system and the governor of New Jersey thought the money was silly because it came from a social networking site?"

"Well, no, but—"

"So there you go," she says, as if a hundred million dollars and the biggest website, like, in the world is equivalent to our school's charity fund-raiser. She finishes packing up her stuff and slings her bag over her shoulder. "Look, Avery, I know it doesn't sound as impressive as selling Livestrong bracelets or even doing a bake sale. But I think we can make a lot of money doing this, and isn't that the bottom line? To raise as much money as we can for the Children's Hospital Boston?"

I think about it. I mean, I guess she's right. And if we make a lot of money, I can totally spin that on my college applications. In fact, maybe I won't even have to mention what the project was! Or maybe I can say something like, *Despite the fact that this project set feminism back by, like, blah-blah years, we were still able to make x number of dollars.*

"Okay," I say, sighing. "Bring on the matchmaking."

four

"SO HOW WILL IT WORK, EXACTLY?" Blake asks me at lunch. Today she brought her tray over to my table and slapped it down right next to me. I guess finding out about the matchmaking service is more important than sitting with Sophie Burns and the popular girls.

And she's not the only one who feels that way. The whole school is totally abuzz. All day people have been coming up to me, asking me for the details. At first I just told the truth—that I didn't know when it was going to start or what was going to happen. But then around third period or so, I just started smiling all mysteriously and being like, "It's getting worked out," which seemed to drive a lot of the girls crazy, especially the eighth graders.

"I'm not sure," I tell Blake honestly. "We'll just have to wait and see."

"It's going to be really fun," Jess says. She squirts ketchup on her hot dog.

"Yeah," Rina chimes in. "Think about it. Everyone's going to end up with their perfect match."

I snort.

"What?" Jess asks. "Why are you scoffing?"

"You really think that the student council charity project is going to end up matching you up with your perfect match?" I take the wrapper off my straw and stick it in my grape juice.

"Yes," Blake says. "Why not?"

"Yeah," Rina says. "You heard what Ms. Tosh said. It's going to be totally scientific."

"Did she say that?" I must have missed that part, since I was kind of in shock.

"Yes," Jess says. "She said it was going to be a totally scientific formula. An algorithm." She says "algorithm" like it's some kind of word that's to be revered or something.

"An algorithm!" Blake squeals. She claps her hands. "That is so cool. I cannot believe she's letting us do this! Your school is way cooler than my old school."

"Come on," I say. "Do you guys really think that some

algorithm that Ms. Tosh came up with is going to predict who your soul mate is? We're thirteen!"

"She didn't come up with it," Jess protests. "She got it off the internet or something."

"Yeah, she researched it," Rina says. She turns to Blake. "Ms. Tosh is, like, a math genius. She went to MIT."

Blake's eyes get superwide.

I unwrap my ham sandwich on organic wheat bread, not quite believing what I'm hearing. Why and how did everyone become so boy crazy? And, more importantly, is there something wrong with me if I'm not?

"I wonder who I'm going to get paired up with," Blake says. Her gaze wanders across the caf to where Sam is sitting at his usual table with Hayden and his other jerky friends.

"Everyone," Rina says, "is going to be wondering who Sam Humphrey gets matched up with."

We all turn and look across the caf.

"Yeah," Blake says. "And only one person can have him."

After school, we have to go look at bridesmaid dresses. There are only, like, three things in the whole world that are worse than going to look at bridesmaid dresses. And right now I can't think of one of them. Besides maybe going to the dentist, but that's only because every time I go, they tell me I'm not allowed to get my braces off yet, and then they tighten them up some more and I can only eat yogurt and pudding for the next three days.

"Ooh, how about this one?" Blake says. She's over in the corner, and she's pulled down some kind of pink monstrosity that has green beading all over it. My mom said we're allowed to pick whatever dresses we want, which is so not fair. I mean, shouldn't there be a color scheme? Or at least some kind of style guideline? My mom says she's too old for everything to be all matchy-matchy, and that she's going to have a simple white dress and simple white tablecloths, and she'll order flowers to match whatever dresses we pick. That's giving us way too much power, I think. I mean, we're only in seventh grade. What do we know about proper wedding attire?

"Um, that one's nice," I say carefully. "But how about this one?" I point to a simple blue dress that's hanging on the rack.

"But it doesn't have any beading," Blake says. "Or lace. Or tulle."

"What's tulle?" I ask. Blake looks at me like I have two heads.

"Here we go, darlings," the saleswoman says, coming out of the back of the store. "Now, what do we think of silver?" She holds up a short, silver sequined dress that looks like something you could end up wearing to Las Vegas.

"Silver?" I glance at my mom, who's sitting over on a bench, flipping through a magazine. "I don't think my mom likes silver." Translation: I don't think I like silver.

"It's fine," my mom says, not even looking up. "You girls can pick out whatever you want." I stare at her. I mean, really. The one time I need her to be a control freak, she doesn't come through.

"Silver would be beautiful," the saleswoman says. I glance at her name tag. Trudy. Figures. Something about the name Trudy makes me think she would definitely favor silver and sequins.

"But what about this dress?" I point to the blue one again. "Don't you think this one would be beautiful?" I twirl around to at least make them think I'm somewhat into this whole dress thing, so that maybe they'll take my opinion seriously.

"Well, that one doesn't even look like a wedding dress," Trudy says.

"But this is a bridal shop!" I say. "All the dresses here are supposed to be for weddings."

"Yes, but some are more weddingy than others," Blake says. Now she's holding up a turquoise (!!) thing that has petticoats or something on the bottom. Petticoats! I mean, I've never even seen petticoats on a dress before. The only reason I know they exist is because I actually pay attention in social studies, and I know all about Civil War attire.

"She's right," Trudy says, nodding. Which is ridiculous, since Blake can't be right since there is no such word as "weddingy."

"Fine," I say, sighing. "I'll try that pink one on."

"Yay!" Blake says.

"Wonderful!" Trudy says.

I mean, how bad can it be?

It looks awful. Actually, not awful on me, if I'm being honest. It's kind of cute on me. The cut of it makes my legs seem superlong, and the way the neckline kind of plunges in the front makes me seem like I might actually have a chest. I sort of like the way I look in it. But the pink and the lace and the just . . . frilliness of it are driving me crazy.

"Um, Blake?" I yell over the dressing room partition. "What do you think?" *Please say you don't like it, please say you don't like it, please say you don't—*

"I love it!" Blake says. She knocks on my dressing room door. "Come out, come out, I want to see." I sigh and then open the door. "We look just like princesses!" she screams, then throws her arms around me. "Can we get them, can we get them?"

"Um . . ." I take a deep breath, but before I can answer her, my mom comes into the dressing area from the front of the store.

"Oh my God," she breathes. "Avery, you look beautiful." She starts to get tears in her eyes. Which kind of settles it. I mean, you can't really say no to a dress that's making the bride cry, especially when the bride is your mother. "You both look just beautiful."

Blake pulls her cell phone out of her purse and starts snapping pics of herself in the full-length mirror. "So are we getting them?"

I look at the dress. I look at my mom. I look at Blake.

"Yes," I say. "Yes, we're getting them." I turn to Trudy. "Wrap them up!"

"It's absolutely gorgeous!" a voice squeals from downstairs. I take my head, drop it in my hands, and lay it down on my desk. When we got home from dress shopping, I came up to my room to do my homework and then finish painting the walls of my—I mean, *our*—room.

I totally thought that Blake would want to help, but she sat down for all of two seconds doing her homework, and then she got a call on her cell phone from SOPHIE BURNS, and the two of them were gabbing away for, like, twenty minutes about the most asinine things, and then Blake invited SOPHIE BURNS over, and now SOPHIE BURNS is here, at our house, downstairs, looking at our dresses.

Well, not our real dresses. I mean, we don't have them yet. We still have to get them fitted. So they're at the store still with Trudy. But Trudy gave us printouts from the catalog, and of course Blake had taken like three million pics on her camera, and so now she and Sophie are downstairs, eating this very delicious trail mix that *I* made, and squealing all over the place.

I had no idea that Sophie and Blake were even such good friends. I mean, the two of them just met yesterday. Who has friends over the day after they meet them? And it's not like I can tell Blake about the history Sophie and I have. She would probably just accuse me of being jealous. Which I am, a little bit. Not of Sophie. But of Sophie being friends with Blake. Sigh.

Gus makes a little growling sound from where he's lying under my desk, and I look down to see him chewing on a stuffed animal. "Poor thing," I say. "You probably have to go out." When she hears the words "go out," Princess pops her little head up from Blake's bed. She has to go out too; she's just a lot more polite about it than Gus is.

I leash them up, yell to my mom that I'm going for a walk, zip up my jacket, and slip out the back door so that I won't run into Sophie and Blake. The air has a slight chill to it, and I inhale the smell of burning leaves that's wafting through my neighborhood. I walk faster, trying to clear my head from the algebra problems and the fact that Sophie Burns is in my kitchen. Gus, surprisingly, is actually behaving, and we make it around the corner with no mishaps.

I'm so lost in my own thoughts that at first I don't realize that someone's calling my name.

"Avery!" I look around, but I don't see anyone, so I keep walking. "Avery!"

I turn around, and as I do, Gus jumps on top of me, leaving two muddy paw prints on the front of my new cream-colored, faux-fur-lined hoodie that I just got a couple of weeks ago. Great. So much for him behaving. "Gus," I say. "Down! I am your pack leader, and you will get down!" Gus cocks his head and looks at me, like *I have no idea what you're talking about and so you sound completely crazy.* Sigh. This would really be a lot easier if he knew English. When he finally jumps down a few seconds later (because he decided he wanted to, not because of anything I did), I see Sam Humphrey running down the driveway of his grandparents' house. Great. First Sophie Burns, now Sam Humphrey. This is like Run into the Popular People Who Annoy You Day. Which is even worse when it falls on the same day as Buy a Pink Frilly Dress Day.

"Hey," he says.

"Hi," I say, looping Gus's leash around my hand. Princess sits down on the sidewalk and looks up at Sam. "If you're looking for Blake, she's not here."

Gus, excited because there's a new person near him, jumps up and onto Sam's chest, leaving two muddy prints that match the ones on my hoodie. I pull on his leash a tiny bit, but not really that hard, because let's face it—Sam Humphrey with muddy paw prints all over his designer sweater is kind of funny.

But Sam doesn't seem to mind. He just kneels down on the ground and starts laughing as Gus licks his face. "You just haven't been trained properly, have you, boy? But we're going to fix that, aren't we?"

Not trained properly? That's not very neighborly.

"He's a rescue dog," I say testily, as Gus finally jumps down and sits on the street, looking up at Sam adoringly. "He's had a very rough life, and he's scared and damaged. And anyway, like I said, Blake isn't here. She's at my house with Sophie Burns, so if you want to go over there and meet them, I'm sure she'd be happy to—"

"Sophie Burns is at your house?"

"Yeah," I say.

He stares at me blankly.

"You know who Sophie Burns is, don't you?"

"Of course I know who Sophie Burns is." He smiles at me. "I just don't like her."

"You don't like Sophie Burns?" I stare at him like he's just announced he's dropping out of school to start his own cattle ranch or something. How can he not like Sophie Burns? It's like a rule that the popular people are all supposed to like each other. Isn't it?

"Do *you* like Sophie Burns?"

"No."

"Then why do you sound surprised that *I* don't like Sophie Burns?"

"Because Sophie Burns is . . . she's . . ."

"She's supposed to be universally liked and revered by everyone?"

"Well, yeah."

"Not me." He shrugs, then reaches down and gives Princess a scratch behind the ears. "So I guess this means Blake ditched me for our training session, huh?"

"I guess so." I didn't know that was, like, a definite thing. He doesn't seem too devastated or anything, which is good for me, since I have no idea why Blake would ditch him. Unless she just forgot? Which makes no sense, since she was looking at him with such longing in the cafeteria today. Well, whatever. It's not really any of my business. Although I probably should get home. Maybe Sophie's gone. Maybe Blake will want to help me finish painting, or maybe we can go over our math homework together. Maybe we can watch DVDs later, or play Wii, or maybe our Netflix on demand subscription will have something good on. Or maybe—

"So do you want to?" Sam's asking.

"Do I want to what?"

"Do you want to stay and hang out? You already have the dogs. We could teach them to sit."

Gus starts drinking out of a mud puddle, and I pull on his collar. "Gus, stop that," I say. "You're going to get sick."

"Looks like he can use all the help he can get, can't you, boy?" Sam asks, grinning.

"I really can't," I say. "I have to get home and finish painting my room." Sam raises his eyebrows, and even though I really don't like him or even care about what he thinks one little bit, even I realize how lame that sounds.

"You have to go home and finish painting your room?"

"Yes," I say defiantly.

"Can't you do that later? I mean, your dog is kind of out of control."

"No, he's not!" I say, as Gus picks that moment to grab the toe of my sneaker and start chewing on it playfully. "He's just getting adjusted to his new surroundings. Like I said, he's had a very hard life."

"Blake said his family had to get rid of him because they had a baby who was allergic."

"Yeah, well, it was very traumatic for him. He's . . . he's obviously sad and going through some post-traumatic stress." Now Gus is tangled up in his leash and barking happily as he tries to untangle himself by lying on the pavement and rolling all around.

"He doesn't look stressed," Sam says. "He looks like a happy dog who was never trained."

"Yes, well, he deals with his stress by playing," I say.

"You couldn't train him right now if you wanted to. He wouldn't respond to any commands, because his head is so messed up and sad."

"Gus," Sam says. "Sit."

Gus immediately gets up from the ground and goes into a sitting position. So does Princess. "He looks trainable to me," Sam says, shrugging. "Come on, let's go into the backyard."

He starts walking up the driveway, and Gus starts following him, and then finally and against my better judgment, when the leash tugs under my hand, I follow him too.

Okay, so it turns out that this is kind of fun. Not, like, amazingly fun or anything, but Sam? He's really smart. And funny. And patient. He didn't even get mad when he was trying to teach Gus to fetch and Gus jumped in his grandparents' pool and then dripped water all over the patio. He just laughed and then got the net and fished out the ball.

And when I, um, stepped in the big water mess and then tracked mud all over his grandparents' kitchen when we went in to get some soda, he still didn't get mad. He just laughed and then cleaned it up with a rag. It was kind of funny, actually. One of the most

popular guys in school cleaning up my muddy foot-
prints. And not even minding.

"So I'm sorry about that whole matchmaking thing,"
he says half an hour or so later. We're sitting in his backyard, on a swing by the garden, while Princess and Gus
run all over the yard, jumping on each other and playing. We figured it was time to end the training session
after the whole pool incident. Gus was doing really well
for a while, though. He was definitely getting the hang
of the whole sitting thing. "I didn't mean to mess up
your plan by giving that survey. It wasn't even my idea.
Hayden thought it would be a good way to get out of science class. And it was."

"That's okay," I say, meaning it. "I mean, Ms. Tosh
is right. Really all that matters is how much money we
raise." And then, as I'm saying it, all of a sudden, out
of nowhere, I start to feel . . . a little weird. I mean, it's
been a very weird day, and now here I am, sitting on
a swing in Sam Humphrey's grandparents' backyard.
With Sam Humphrey. It's pretty crazy when you think
about it. And it's getting dark and I should really be
heading home, even though I texted my mom to tell
her where I was. She's probably getting dinner ready,
and she might need my help even though she has
Will to help her now, and I really should go mostly so

that I don't have to think about the fact that my stomach is getting kind of sparkly, which makes no sense because—

"There you are!" a voice comes trilling from the front of the yard, and I look over and see Blake tromping through the gate and into the backyard, Sophie Burns trailing behind her.

I jump up like I've been caught doing something wrong, even though I haven't. I mean, yeah, maybe we were sitting a little close, but we were just talking about and playing with the dogs. And I don't even like Sam. My sparkly stomach means nothing. Just a moment of temporary insanity.

"Hey, guys!" I yell, a little too brightly. "Hey, Blake and Sophie! Look, Sam, it's Blake and Sophie!"

"Ewww," Sophie says. "Whose dog is that?" Gus is jumping all over her, his muddy paws ruining her jeans and sneakers. "He smells like moldy socks."

"It's my dog," I say. "And socks can't get moldy."

"Gus, sit," Sam says. But Gus doesn't sit. He just keeps jumping all over.

"I guess that move needs some work," I say. Sam looks at me. I look at Sam. We both burst out laughing.

"What does that mean?" Blake says. I notice that she's

wearing something different from what she was wearing at home, which means she changed before coming over to Sam's. Now she's wearing skinny jeans tucked into soft, caramel-colored boots, and a baggy black sweater. I look down at my muddy hoodie and suddenly feel like a total mess.

"It means that we've been working with Gus for, like, an hour, and he still doesn't know how to sit," Sam says. "But that's okay. We're going to keep at it."

Something about the way Blake looks at me then, her eyes kind of cool and a little scary, makes me think that she doesn't really appreciate Sam calling me and him a "we." But it's not my fault! We're *not* a "we," I don't even like him like that. In fact, I don't even really like him at all. He's stuck-up and arrogant, and he flirts with everyone.

Of course, he hasn't been stuck-up and arrogant to me. And he hasn't tried to flirt with me either. Oh, God. Why hasn't he tried to flirt with me? Am I that hideous? Is it the mud that Gus tracked all over me? Is—

"So why'd you guys start without me?" Blake wants to know. She's keeping her tone light, but you can tell she's kind of annoyed.

"We didn't," I say. "I was just taking the dogs for a walk and Sam saw me."

"Eww," Sophie says again. "Blake, your dog, like, seriously needs a bath."

"He's not even that smelly," I say, rolling my eyes. I mean, seriously. Drama much? "And besides, he fell in a pool."

"And he has post-traumatic stress disorder," Sam chimes in. And then he winks at me.

"And he's not my dog," Blake says. "He's Avery's dog."

"Come here, Gus," I say. Miraculously, he trots over and then flops on the grass at my feet.

"Anyway," Blake says, "we're here to train the dogs. Or, I mean, my dog. We're here to train Princess." She yells over to Princess, who's lounging under a big fir tree behind the swing.

We all hang out for a while longer, playing with the dogs, but for some reason, it's definitely not as fun with Blake and Sophie there. Probably because I'm constantly worried about what Sophie thinks, or if Gus is going to embarrass me by doing something to her. And I'll admit I'm still a little thrown by the weird feeling I had in my stomach when Sam and I were sitting so close.

Later, after Sophie's mom comes and picks her up from Sam's, and Blake and I are walking home with our dogs, she says, "So you like Sam now?"

I look over at her, shocked, but she's not looking at

me, she's just staring straight ahead, putting one foot in front of the other, her face blank.

"No!" I say, shaking my head. "I was just walking the dogs and he came out. He was looking for you."

She glances at me, and her face softens a little. "Do you swear?"

"I swear!" I say. I'm about to add that Sam is, you know, not my type, and then start getting into the one million reasons why that is, but something tells me bagging on the guy she likes isn't going to go help when it comes to us becoming BFFs. Not to mention the matter of the weird stomach sparkliness, but since I've decided that was a total fluke and a big mistake, I don't really think it's worth bringing up.

"What did he say exactly?" Blake asks, grabbing my arm. "Tell me everything."

"He asked where you were," I say, struggling to remember. Did he say that? Or was it only after I said Blake wasn't with me that he asked about her? He definitely said he thought she'd ditched him, and that def counts as looking for her, right?

"Yeah, but how did he say it?" Blake asks.

"What do you mean?"

"I mean was he, like, longing for me to be there? Or was it just, like, kind of casual?"

"I think it was casual," I say, still trying to remember. Her face falls, so I quickly add, "But it was more like he was *trying* to be casual about it than he actually *was* casual about it, you know what I mean?"

She nods slowly, and then smiles. "More like he was trying to pretend that he didn't want me to be there, because he was playing hard to get!"

"Totally!" I say. Of course, I'm not exactly sure that's what was going on, but really, is there any harm in letting the poor girl think that? Besides, maybe he *was* playing hard to get. That Sam is very crafty. Look at how fast he whipped Gus into shape.

"Thanks, Avery," she says, and squeezes my hand. It's almost enough to make me forgive her for the bridesmaid dresses, and for bringing Sophie Burns to our house.

Until the next morning. Which is when Sophie Burns accosts me as soon as I get off the bus. We're walking into school, kids jostling into us and everyone trying to be the first one through the doors. Which really makes no sense, since once they're actually inside, they spend all their time waiting to get out.

"Hi, Avery," she says. Her platform heels fall into step with my sneakers, and I glance at her out of the corner of my eye, suddenly very nervous. Sophie Burns makes it a point not to speak to me. Like, ever. In fact, until yesterday, when she started telling me Gus was a smelly, disgusting creature, she hasn't talked to me since she stopped being friends with me. Unless you count the time when she brought this superexpensive Dior cardigan to school, and then draped it over her chair in the cafeteria (which was ridiculous, since it's always super cold in there, and so it made no sense that she was taking her cardigan off—it was totally only because she wanted everyone to notice it, which, of course, everyone did). I was sitting in the seat behind her, and I got my chair leg stuck on it, and of course she couldn't just say, "Excuse me, you're on my sweater," like a normal person, she had to scream, "GET OFF MY SWEATER. DON'T YOU KNOW HOW MUCH IT COST?" I mean, seriously.

"Hi, Sophie," I say now. "If you're looking for Blake, she got a ride to school with her dad."

Blake was running late this morning because her alarm went off twenty minutes late (the truth was she just kept hitting snooze), and then it was her turn to walk Gus and Princess. Not to mention Blake has a very complicated morning beauty routine. So Will said he'd take her.

"Actually," Sophie says, "I was looking for you."

"You were?"

"Yeah," she says. "I heard that you're in charge of the matchmaking project."

"I am," I say. "And no, I'm not sure when we're going to have the questionnaires ready. Probably by the end of the day, but there are no guarantees."

"Thanks, Avery," she says, giving me a big smile. "Just let me know when you hear something."

Her tone sounds all syrupy sweet, but I'm smart enough to know that it's totally fake. She's obviously just using me because she wants the inside scoop on what's happening with the matchmaking. She might even want me to fix the results or something, that's how conniving she is.

Well, I will not drop to her level. I will not pretend to even be nice to her. Who cares if she's friends with Blake now? Who cares if she and I used to be friends until she got all popular and dropped me? I really do not need to be sucked back into her craziness. In fact, I'm not even going to tell her anything more about the matchmaking project. Last year, when we were still friends, I asked her if she wanted to be on student council, and of course she said no. If she'd said yes, if she cared about something more than her dumb Dior cardigan, maybe she'd be involved. Maybe she'd know what was going on.

"So, Avery," she says. "Do you want to sit with me and Blake at lunch? We have a lot of catching up to do."

I open my mouth. Then close it. Open it. Close it. And then finally, before I even realize what I'm saying, I squeak, "Okay."

Whatever. It's not like I sold out or anything. I mean, Sophie and I *used* to be friends. Best friends. So it's just like two old friends sitting together. And I know I said I wanted nothing to do with her, but one lunch doesn't mean that we're going to become friends again. She probably just wants to catch up, to ask me what's been going on in my life. I'll ask her how her older brother is doing at his college in Connecticut, and if her mom's entered any of those pie-making competitions lately, and if her dad's golf game is improving. And she'll ask me about my mom's wedding and what it's going to be like to have a stepsister, and then we'll talk about how we just grew apart, and that will be that. It's like closure.

"She totally wants to weasel her way back in with you!" Rina says. It's second-period gym, and we're supposed to be running around the track as a warm-up, but Rina and I are more like speed walking. Seriously, gym class is a pretty big joke. Our teacher, Coach Randall, doesn't even care if you walk or not. That's because he's more into the boys' wrestling team. He makes us run around the track for the first ten minutes of class, and then he splits us up into teams and makes us play the sport of his choice. Today it's going to be kickball. Kickball! Tell me whoever got in wonderful shape playing kickball? I mean, come on. Not that it really matters. I mean, by the time we're done with the stupid warm-up, we only have about twenty minutes left of class before we have to go in and change anyway. I should totally start a petition or something to revamp physical education in this school. Physically fit bodies are the only way you can have a physically fit mind. I forget who said that, but I think it was some kind of totally famous philosopher like Aristotle or Galileo or something.

"She doesn't want to get back in with me," I say to Rina. We're getting ready to pass Coach Randall, so we pick up the pace just a little bit into a slow jog. Not that he really cares, but if you go right by him and you're walking, he'll yell, "Girls! This isn't the Bombay Walking Club for Old Women! Get a move on!" Which makes no sense, since Bombay is in India and I've never heard of them having a walking club for old women. Unless it's something more local. I'll have to Google it.

Rina looks at me, her eyebrows raised. "She asked you to sit with her at lunch."

"So?"

"So, she asked you that right after she found out you were in charge of the matchmaking project!"

"So what?"

"So! That obviously means that she wants to get back into your good graces!"

We go around the curve in the track and slow our pace. The laces of my sneakers are slapping against my shoe. "Hold on," I say. "I have to retie my laces."

I crouch down on the track, and Rina crouches down next to me, pretending to tie her laces too.

"Where is Blake, anyway?"

"I don't know," I say. "I haven't seen her all day." The coach blows the whistle, and we line up, getting ready to pick teams for kickball.

"So what are you going to do?" Rina asks as we walk through the grass toward the field.

"About what?"

"About Sophie," she says. "Are you going to sit with her?"

"Are you going to be mad at me if I do?"

She bites her lip and then squints out across the field, thinking about it. "No," she says.

"Because you're a good friend?"

"Because sometimes people have to learn their lesson the hard way."

On my way out of the locker room, I run into Sam in the hall.

"Hey," he says, pulling my ponytail. I instantly wish I'd run a brush through my hair. Yeah, we don't do that much activity in gym, but we do enough to get our hair messed up. I wonder why I care, and why I got a little flush of pleasure when he pulled my hair. It's definitely *not* because I want him to flirt with me or anything. It's probably just because the fact that he *is* flirting with me makes me feel a little more normal. Like I'm not just some loser who doesn't deserve to be flirted with.

"Hi," I say. "Um, Blake's not here. I don't know where she is. I mean, she was supposed to be coming in late, but I haven't seen her."

"That sucks," he says, not sounding like he really cares. He's wearing this really soft-looking blue sweater that brings out the blue in his eyes. "So, listen," he says. "We're having a special meeting of student council."

"When?" I ask, struggling to keep the stack of books I'm carrying from falling over. My locker is on the other side of the school, so after gym I always end up having to carry around books for all my morning classes. So annoying.

"At lunch," Sam says. He falls into step with me, then reaches over and takes my books out of my hands. I'm about to protest, but he swings them up under his arm like they're nothing. "Apparently the matchmaking service thing has been such a hit that Ms. Tosh wants to get started on it right away. So we're going to be picking the questions we want to use and putting the questionnaire together today."

"I thought she said she had some scientific formula or something?"

"I guess not," he says. He grins, and my stomach does another sparkly flip. *Stop*, I tell myself. *You can't just start going all crazy every time some guy smiles at you. You're going to become just as bad as Sophie.* Not that guys smile at me all the time. Okay, like, hardly ever. Okay, fine, never, unless you count the guy who works behind the meat counter at Stop & Shop, which I don't, since he smiles at everyone, including two-year-olds and old ladies. Plus, he's in college. And I never feel this way when that guy smiles at me.

"So I'll see you there?" Sam says, as we stop outside my classroom. He hands me my books.

"Yeah," I say. "See you there." I pull out my phone and send a text to Blake. WHERE R U? But by the time the meeting rolls around, she still hasn't texted me back.

five

WE HOLD THE STUDENT COUNCIL MEETING
in the green room of our school, which is actually
just this big theater room that they call the green
room because it's painted green. It's a huge, wide-
open space between two hallways that has stadium
seating and a projector at the front. Which makes
it perfect for meetings, film screenings, that kind of
stuff. The only bad thing about it is the green. I know
it's my fave color, but this green is not a nice sea
foam, or even a deep hunter. It's like a yellowy, puke
green.

"I always wondered what came first," Sam says.
"Like, did they want this to be called the green room,
and then they painted it green? Or did they paint it
green and then just start calling it the green room?" He

pauses and looks around. For some reason, Sam has decided to sit right next to me.

"They obviously called it the green room *after* they painted," I say. I pull my notebook out of my bag, turn to a fresh page, and write *Possible Ideas for Questions to Ask on the Matchmaking Questionnaire*. When we got here a few minutes ago, Ms. Tosh told us we should take a few minutes to brainstorm, and then we'd go over everyone's ideas as a group.

"You think?"

"Yeah, because, otherwise, they would have picked a better color green. It's like they're making fun of it. Also this really isn't even a greenroom. It should be called a theater room or a screening room, but they probably didn't have those terms when the school was built."

Sam nods. "Makes sense."

I twirl my pen between my fingers and try to think of something I would want to ask my potential soul mate. Something that would be a determining factor in keeping us apart or together.

Finally I write, *Do you recycle?*

"Do you recycle?" Sam asks.

"What?" I look up in shock and drop my pen. It goes rolling down the big stadium stairs of the green room.

"Do you recycle," he says. "That's what you wrote on your paper." He points to where I wrote it.

"First of all," I say, pulling another pen out of my bag, "you shouldn't be looking at my paper. This isn't a group activity."

He looks around the room, where pretty much everyone has their desks pushed near other people's, murmuring in low tones about what they should write. At the front of the room, Ms. Tosh is grading papers, looking up every so often and giving us a satisfied look, like we're doing great work and not just coming up with some dumb questions about soul mates that won't even matter since we're only thirteen and no one meets their soul mate when they're thirteen. And that's even assuming you believe in things like soul mates, which I'm not sure I do.

"Trust me," he says. "If I wanted to steal an idea, it wouldn't be a question about recycling."

"Why not?" I say. I write, *Do you do your best to save trees?* on my paper. "Recycling is very important to the environment."

"Yeah, but . . ." He frowns. "Do you really think that you'd only date a guy who recycles?"

"Yes," I say.

"Then I guess I'd be out of the running," he says, smirking.

"I guess so." I shrug. Figures he doesn't recycle.

"Look, there's nothing wrong with wanting a guy who recycles," he says. "But you should add some other, more personal questions too."

"Recycling *is* personal," I say. It is to me, at least. How could I ever like a boy who doesn't recycle? If he doesn't respect the planet, then how do I know he's going to respect me? It really makes perfect sense when you think about it.

"There must be something else that you value," he says. "What about dogs? Is it important that the guy you like likes dogs?"

"No," I say.

"No?"

"No."

"Why not?"

"Because *I* don't like dogs!"

"You don't like dogs?" He looks at me like I'm crazy. "But you have a dog!"

"I know, but I didn't want one." This whole conversation is getting a little out of control, and I really don't feel like I should be explaining to him about how I ended up at the animal shelter because of Blake, and how since then she's shown, like, no interest in being a dog owner. "Look, I don't want to get into it," I say.

"Fine," he says. "I'll stop bothering you."

"Good."

"Good."

He turns back to his own list, and I tap my pencil against my paper, wondering what else I should write. What's your favorite color? What kind of music do you like? Those seem kind of lame, but since I'm in charge of the project, I don't think I can really get away with just writing down two questions, both of them having to do with the environment. Everyone knows that in order to be a good leader, you need to be well rounded.

I sneak a glance over at what Sam's writing. *Would you rather spend your free time at a party, or spend a quiet night in watching a movie?* Hmm. I guess that makes sense. I mean, you'd want to make sure that the person you were dating would want to spend their time the same way you do.

But it would be totally copying to write that down, so instead I write, *Would you rather spend your Saturday afternoon at a movie, or playing paintball?*

We spend so much time writing down our questions that, at the end, Ms. Tosh doesn't even have time to go over them with us. She just collects all our papers and says that she'll pick her favorites and make up the questionnaires, which we'll get in homeroom tomorrow.

Which isn't really fair, since I'm the one who's supposed to be in charge of everything, but whatever. There will be plenty of work to do when it comes to tabulating the results and distributing them to everyone. I'm out of the meeting and on my way to sixth-period math class when Blake comes flying down the hall.

"Where have you been?" I ask. "Didn't you get the text I sent you? I was worried! No one told me you were going to be this late. Where were you?"

"I had to wash my black shirt," she says. "And it took forever."

I stare at her. "You're late because you were washing a shirt?"

Geez. Definitely whoever Blake gets matched up with is going to have to be interested in fashion.

"Yeah," she says. "But it doesn't matter anymore."

"What doesn't?"

"Everything! Nothing!"

"Okay, you kind of sound like a crazy person," I say.

"Come into the bathroom with me," she says. "And I'll tell you."

"But the bell's about to ring," I say. "Can you text me?"

"Avery," she says, "I am having a horrible day and I need to talk to you. Now, can you come into the bathroom or not?"

I hesitate. This is going to sound totally lame, but I've never been late to a class before. Like, ever. And I don't really want to start now. On the other hand, in a couple of weeks, Blake is going to be my sister. The only sister I've ever had. And she's also going to maybe be my best friend. So I really have no choice, do I?

"Yes," I say. "I'll go into the bathroom with you."

We walk down the hall superfast, mostly because we don't want to get caught not being in class (I don't actually know for sure if that's why we're walking so fast, but I'm assuming that when one's doing something wrong, one moves faster so they don't get caught), and I'm so nervous that I'm not really watching where I'm going, which is why I go slapping right into Sophie Burns.

"Oh!" I say. Her books go flying out of her hands and onto the ground, and I automatically stoop down to help pick them up, before I remember that

1. it's Sophie Burns, and
2. I hate her.

"Watch where you're going!" she says. "You can't just come barreling down the hall like some kind of crazed lunatic."

"I wasn't barreling," I say, rolling my eyes at her. And seriously, that's the best she could come up with? I'm totally reminded about what a brat she is, and I'm glad I had a student council meeting during lunch, since I might have weakened and actually sat with her, which would have a been a huge mistake.

"Whatever," she says. She's wearing this really cute ruffly black-and-white blouse with a black pencil skirt and heels. One day a week, Sophie and her friends dress up. They think it makes them special or something. They make sure to coordinate outfits, too. Like, they'll go to the store and each get a certain piece that has the same pattern or color. They started doing it after she stopped being friends with me, so I was never really involved.

Sophie turns to Blake. "Sorry again about the party. It just wouldn't work, you know?" She gives her a sad smile, then turns around and trills, "Toodles!" over her shoulder.

"Did she just say 'toodles'?" I ask as she swishes down the hall. "That's definitely new. She never said 'toodles' when we were—"

But Blake has my hand and she's pulling me down the hallway toward the bathroom.

She goes in and slams the door behind her. "Did you hear her?"

"Yeah, she said 'toodles.'" I'm still wondering how someone could be so ridiculous.

"No!" Blake says. "Not that! About the party!"

"Sort of," I say. "Something about how she was sorry it didn't work out?" I reach into my bag and pull out my hairbrush, and start running it through my hair. I brushed it before the student council meeting, but for some reason, it's all sticking up again.

"Yes!" Blake says. "They're having a surprise sleepover party for Kaci Mitchell in a few weeks." Right. Kaci Mitchell. Sophie's best friend and second in command of the populars.

"So . . ."

"So! This morning Sophie texted me and said, 'I'm so sorry you won't be able to come to the party, but the list is full.'"

"What list?" I ask.

"The list! Like, the guest list?" The guest list? For a slumber party?

"Oh. Well, maybe Kaci's mom said that she could only have a certain number of people or something."

"The party's at Sophie's! And she told me last night I could come."

I hear the bell ringing through the bathroom door, but I'm totally not even thinking about it. "Are you *serious?*" I say. "God, she is a real piece of work." I wonder if I should tell Blake about Sophie, about how she and I used to be friends. I wonder if I should warn her, if now that Sophie's being a brat to her, she'll realize that I'm not just being jealous. "Blake, listen," I say. "I have to tell you something. Sophie—"

"Ohmigod!" Blake twirls around from the sink. Her face, which just a minute ago was the picture of despair, is now lit up with excitement.

"What?" I ask. "What is it?"

"We can have a party!" she says. "A boy/girl party!"

"A party?" I ask, thinking about it. I mean, if she wants to have a party at our house, I guess that would be okay. We have a huge family room that's pretty good for sleepovers. I mean, we definitely can't sleep in my room, there are too many unfinished walls. Although I guess we could finish painting tonight, and then Rina and Jess could put their sleeping bags— Wait a minute. "Wait a minute, what did you say?"

"A boy/girl party!" She sounds really giddy and excited, and my eye does a twitch.

"You want to have a *boy/girl party?* At *our house?* Are you crazy?"

"No," she says. "We have to! It'll be fun."

"What about a sleepover?" I try. "We could have Rina

and Jess over, and didn't you make some friends in your
math class? We could maybe ask if we could have a fire
in the fire pit in the backyard, and we could make s'mores
and tell scary stories and—"

"No." Blake shakes her head back and forth. "It has to
be a boy/girl party."

"Why?"

"Because that's the only way we're ever going to
upstage Sophie!" She says it like she's trying to explain
something really simple to a child who's just not getting
it. Then she reaches into her bag and pulls out a pair of
fishnet stockings.

"What are those?"

"Just tights," she says, shrugging.

"Oh," I say, even though they're not really "just tights."
They have this really crazy pattern on them, and when
paired with her skirt that's just a little bit too short, she
looks like she's in eighth or ninth grade. I'm not sure if
I should be worried or jealous. I'm a little bit of both. "If
your dad won't let you wear those, I don't think he'll let
you have a boy/girl party."

"No," she says. "Probably not." Oh, thank God. She's
finally starting to see the light. And then she smiles.
"But your mom will."

six

THERE'S NO LAW OR ANYTHING THAT says I have to do this. I don't *have* to ask my mom if I can have a boy/girl party. I mean, that's kind of super embarrassing. I've never even expressed any interest in boys before. Not even close. So how am I supposed to convince her I want to have a boy/girl party? Especially when I *don't* really want to. I think about this all through the rest of the day, and finally I decide that even if I do want to become BFFs with Blake, it doesn't mean that I have to do everything she says. Part of any friendship and/or sisterhood is a good give-and-take.

"Pass the meatballs," I say to Will later that night, when we're all at the table having a good old-fashioned family dinner. My mom is so psyched we're all eating together that she can hardly contain herself.

"So what did you girls do at school today?" Will asks.

"Nothing," I say. "Well, actually, I'm working on the student council charity project." I grab the parmesan cheese and sprinkle it onto my spaghetti. My mom's been so busy with wedding stuff that I haven't even had a chance to tell her. "I got picked to run the whole thing."

"Avery!" my mom says. "That is absolutely amazing! They hardly ever pick seventh graders, do they? What's the fund-raiser going to be?"

"She's going to be hooking people up," Blake says, reaching across the table and grabbing the bowl of salad.

"No, I'm not!" I say. "It's . . . it's a matchmaking service, but it's totally scientific." Well, as scientific as you can be when the questions are being thought up by seventh and eighth graders who have no experience with finding their soul mates.

Blake kicks me under the table. "Ow!" I say. "What the heck was—"

She looks at me and raises her eyebrows. "Ask her!" she mouths.

I give her a confused look, like I can't tell what she's saying. La, la, la. What party? I don't remember anything about a party, la la la. "So anyway," I babble, "we're going to be matching up everyone who fills out our questionnaire with the person in the school they're most compatible with."

"You girls are too young to be thinking about boys," Will says. I send him a silent thank-you. Blake glares at him and then spears her meatball so hard that it flies off her fork and falls on the floor. Gus quickly shuffles over and wolfs it down. Hmm. I hope his stomach can handle that. In just the time I've been home from school he's eaten the rest of a ham sandwich that was left over from my lunch, a package of turkey bacon that I gave him so he would stop whining, two bones, and a yellow sock. Well, he didn't eat the sock. He just chewed on it until I grabbed it, and then we played tug of war for, like, twenty minutes until the sock ripped. I hope Will doesn't mind. It was his sock.

"Oh, we're not thinking about boys," I say. "It's a project for charity. You have to pay five dollars to get your results, and then we're going to donate the money to Children's Hospital Boston."

"I'm helping her," Blake says. Which isn't really true, but whatever. If it keeps me from having to bring up the potential boy/girl party, then we can pretend she's helping.

"That's great," my mom says. "I was always tempted to try one of those matchmaking internet dating sites."

Will raises his eyebrows and looks amused. "You were?"

"Yes, before I met you." My mom reaches over and takes Will's hand, and they gaze at each other the way people do when they're in love. I try not to gag.

"*Anyway*," Blake says, obviously desperate to get the conversation back on topic. "It's been really hard meeting people, which is why I decided to join student council."

"Oh, honey," Will says, "you'll make friends in no time. You just had that girl Sophie over here last night." Will is obviously kind of clueless when it comes to middle-school politics, otherwise he would have taken one look at Sophie's manicured nails and curled hair and Michael Kors jeans and he would have known that she was not the type of friend that becomes your BFF.

My mom's a little more with-it, and she knows about my history with Sophie, so she just gives a tight smile.

"Yeah, but it's still been hard making friends," Blake says pointedly. She looks at me. "I wish there was something we could do where we could get a big group of people together so I could meet everyone."

"Yeah," I say. "Me too. Oh, well, I guess it will just take time." Gus is licking my hand under the table, so I pull a strand of spaghetti off my plate and slip it to him. He gobbles it down and then keeps licking. Sam definitely would not like that I just did that. He'd totally think I was teaching Gus that if he licks my hand, he gets rewarded with food. Which I definitely have, since Gus is licking it again. But if I don't give him food, how will I get him to stop licking? It's like a vicious cycle.

"You mean like a party?" Will asks, suddenly getting in touch with his inner thirteen-year-old girl.

"That would be fun!" my mom says. "You haven't had a party in a while, hon."

"You mean like a sleepover?" I ask, deciding to plant this idea in my mom's head before Blake can start talking about the ridiculousness that is the boy/girl party.

"Sure," my mom says. "You guys can roast marshmallows in the backyard."

"Sounds fun," I say. God, me and my mom are so in sync. Blake kicks me under the kitchen table again.

"Ow!"

My mom and Will look at me.

"You know who's nice?" Blake says. "That kid Sam who lives around the corner. He was helping us train Gus and Princess yesterday."

My mouth drops open. She didn't even care about training the dogs yesterday! In fact, she showed up late and then hardly even worked with them. She just flipped her hair around and did a lot of giggling.

"Sam Humphrey?" my mom says. "Yes, he seems like a nice boy. His grandmother runs her own catering service. I'm thinking of using her for the wedding. Apparently she specializes in last-minute affairs."

"What boy?" Will asks, putting his fork down. He sounds like maybe he wants to kill Sam, even though he doesn't know him. Yikes.

"He's just this boy who lives around the corner," I say, like Sam is about as inconsequential as, well, anything. "Actually, he doesn't even live there. His grandparents do, but he visits them a lot. Anyway, can we rent a movie for the sleepover?"

"Of course," my mom says.

Suddenly Blake stares down at her plate and then bursts out crying.

"What's wrong?" Will asks, reaching over and squeezing her shoulder. "Honey, why are you crying?"

"I just . . . I just . . ." She's sniffling so hard she can hardly talk. Princess walks over and sets her head down on Blake's lap, and Gus starts licking her leg for some reason. Like that's going to make her feel better. Sigh.

"Blake, what's wrong?" I ask. She can't really be this upset about Sophie, can she? Although I was pretty upset when Sophie decided to freeze me out at the beginning of the year. It was kind of traumatic, if you want to know the truth. But I got over it, and Blake will too. Except when I think about it, I guess I'm not exactly over it.

I mean, if I were *really* over it, I wouldn't be thinking about her so much. Not that I think about her a lot, but she definitely affects my life sometimes, like how she's now trying to be friends with my soon-to-be stepsister and how that totally bothers me. Maybe I should have warned Blake. I should have told her about Sophie, about her history. But I thought Blake would just think I was being jealous. And it's really not my place to—

"It's my birthday!" Blake wails.

"Your birthday?" I had no idea! How horrible! I almost missed my own sister's birthday. My mom really needs to get better about being on top of this stuff. The wedding is just making her go all floopy. Who knows what kind of other important events we've missed?

"Yeah." Blake sniffs. "It's in a week. And I really was hoping I could have a . . . a . . . a big party because I miss my friends at home!" She blows her nose on her napkin. "But the only people I really know here are Sam and Avery," Blake says, obviously completely forgetting about Sophie. "Maybe the three of us could all do something special." Oh, yeah, sounds fun. Not.

"Of course," my mom says, and reaches over, taking Blake's hand.

"What do you mean 'something special'?" I ask suspiciously.

"Maybe we could all watch a movie in the rec room," Blake says.

"You and Avery are not going to be left alone with some boy," Will says.

"He's not really 'some boy,'" I say, before I realize what I'm doing. "I mean, I've known him since I was five."

"Well, he's not coming over," Will says.

"Oooohhhhh!" Blake wails. Her small shoulders start shaking with sobs, but now I'm beginning to wonder if she's faking this whole thing. I watch her face carefully for signs of acting, but if she is, she's really good at it.

"Of course Sam can come over," my mom says, shooting Will a look. "In fact, why don't you girls have a party?"

Blake blinks, like it's the first time she's thought of it. "A party?" she says.

"Yeah, a birthday party," my mom says. "You can invite Sam and whoever else you want."

"I guess that could be fun," Blake says doubtfully. Oh, for the love of God.

"A boy/girl party?" Will says.

"Just some friends," my mom says firmly. "Whoever Blake wants."

Will looks like he wants to say something else, but my mom gives him another one of her looks, and so he shuts up. And then Blake blows her nose again and my mom gets up to serve the strawberry shortcake and I guess we're having a boy/girl party.

Okay, so the thing is, I kind of maybe dropped the ball on that whole party thing. I mean, I *did* tell Blake that I would ask my mom. And if I wasn't going to do it, I shouldn't have told her that I would, you know? I mean, that's lying. This is what I'm thinking about while I'm standing at the bus stop the next morning. I have a lot of time to think about it too, because I'm just standing here by myself. Not talking to Blake. And that's because, um, she's kind of mad at me.

Our conversation last night, a summary:

Blake: What the heck was that?

Me (dips paintbrush in green paint and smears it on wall): What was what?

Blake: You were supposed to ask your mom about the party!

Me: I know, but I just . . . I don't know, I chickened out. But it turned out okay,

you're getting the party, yay! Now do
you want to help me paint?

Blake: No. (Walks over to computer and
starts designing invitations for her birthday
party. Doesn't talk to me for the rest of
the night. Or this morning, even though I
totally asked her if she wanted some raisin
toast, which I guess she didn't.)

Anyway. Now we're standing at the bus stop, and it's
totally silent. She and I are definitely not off to a good
start when it comes to us becoming friends.

"Hey, Blake," I try. "You know what could be fun? We
could go to the party store after school and look at some
decorations."

"Maybe," she says, glancing at me out of the corner
of her eye. Then she goes back to looking at her cell.
Geez. I remind myself that I have to be nice to Blake
even when she's being a little testy, since there's no
way this can be an easy transition for her. I mean,
think about how horrible it would be if I had to move
to New York City and start a whole new school in
the middle of the year. I would be freaking out. And
besides, I really shouldn't have told her I would ask

about the boy/girl party if I wasn't going to follow through. I try to think of something that would make Blake not so mad at me. Something I could do for her that would be nice. Something she would really want, something . . .

And then it hits me: Sam. I can make sure she gets matched up with him on the matchmaking project.

It's not really against the rules. I mean, it is but it isn't. It is in the sense that I don't think (okay, I know) that I'm not supposed to be doing it. Manipulating the matches, I mean. Like I said, who really thinks they're going to get matched up with their soul mate in the seventh or eighth grade? Not to mention that we're the ones who came up with the questions, which makes it even more unlikely that these matches mean anything. So really, even though I'm technically doing something wrong, it's not like it really *matters*.

Still. In homeroom, when Mr. Hunter passes out the questionnaires, I feel myself getting all nervous. I look around guiltily, like maybe someone in here can tell that I have a plan to, like, overthrow the student council. Although it's not overthrowing, exactly. I mean, it's more like just, uh, messing with the results. If this were like an election or something, I'd probably get killed. At least arrested. It's scary, but I also feel kind of excited, too. It's like a rebellion for what I believe is right.

I look down at my paper.

Question one: If you could spend the night watching a movie or going out and playing paintball, what would you pick? I guess Ms. Tosh picked one of my questions. Yay! I fill in the little bubble for (a) staying home and watching a movie.

I wonder what everyone else is writing. What if I'm the only one who picked staying home to watch a movie? And everyone else wants to go out and play paintball and now I'm, like, a freak or something? What if I go to match everyone up, and it turns out that I have no match? Yeah, I think this whole exercise is kind of pointless, but I don't want to be the only one who doesn't have a match. That would be completely humiliating. Especially since you just know that later today everyone's going to be running around, asking who they got matched with, and someone is bound to ask me, and then what will I say? I'm getting myself really worked up, into kind of a panic even, until I remember that it doesn't matter if no one matches me. Because I'm in charge of the matches! I can match myself up with whoever I want!

I decide it should be Kevin Hudson, definitely. I glance over at him out of the corner of my eye and watch as he moves down the paper, neatly filling in circles. I notice he's picked that he would stay home and watch a movie too. I feel relieved that someone else wanted to stay in. Playing paintball is actually kind of scary. I've never played before, but Sophie's brothers used to all the time, and one time one of them came home with this huge bruise on his leg that was pretty disgusting. Paintball is one of those activities that should definitely be outlawed or banned, or at least regulated with some kind of age limit. I mean, really.

"Three more minutes," Mr. Hunter says from the front of the room. "And then you'll have to turn in your questionnaires."

Yikes. I've hardly even started mine. Not that it matters. I quickly fill in the rest of the questions, answering as best I can (except the one about how important fashion is to you. That one I kind of lied about, because I didn't want to admit that it isn't really important at all, because the truth is, it kind of is, at least a little, even though it kind of shouldn't be, which made the question kind of confusing and a little bit of a gray area, but oh well), and then pass it up front.

Taylor Meachum, the kid who sits in front of me, takes my questionnaire from me and immediately starts to read it.

"Hey," I say, "those questionnaires are private."

"I can read it if I want," he says. Taylor Meachum is really kind of a jerk. One time in the fifth grade he brought in this jar of paint that he swore was temporary hair dye and gave everyone red and blue streaks in their hair, and it totally wasn't washable and all the parents had to come and pick up their kids and then, like, wash them in turpentine or something equally disgusting.

"No, you can't," I say. "That's official government property."

"It's not official government property," he says, rolling his eyes.

"Yes, it is," I say. "It's property of the student government, which is governed by the same privacy laws as any government at the local, state, and/or national level."

I'm not completely sure if that's true, but there's no way I want him to see that I'd rather stay home than play paintball. I'm not sure he believes me, but he passes them up front anyway.

All morning, it's kind of like I'm a celebrity.

The things that are said to me, a summary:

Sophie Burns: Hey, Avery, when are you going to match everyone up? Do you

think they'll be ready by lunch? Because
we should totally sit together! I could even
help you if you need it. Did I tell you I'm
having a sleepover?

Jessica Partridge: Avery! OHMIGOD,
like, I just found out that Jeremy Givens
put down the same exact answers as me
for, like, seven questions! Do you think
that's going to be enough to match us up??

Hannah Michaels: Hello! Are you even
listening to me, Avery? I need to know the
exact moment the results are going on sale,
so that I can be the first one in line. Are
they giving out, like, bracelets or anything?
You know, to hold your place in line?

Seriously, the whole school has gone completely
crazy. Even Jess and Rina are getting into it, asking if
it would be okay to get their results first, since we're all
going to be running the booth at lunch where students
can come up and pay their money to find out who they
got matched with.

By the time third period rolls around, I'm totally fried.

I have no idea how the popular kids do it, being the center of attention all day every day. It's very exhausting. I have a special pass to get out of math class and meet with Ms. Tosh in the computer lab, where I guess we're going to be going through all the questionnaires and making up the matches.

"Hi, Avery," she says when she sees me. She's wearing this really cool white wool skirt that looks supersoft, a pair of thick black tights, and a long sweater over a thin pink tunic. Ms. Tosh is kind of a fashionista, but in one of those ways that's almost over everyone's head. Like, she doesn't just wear what you can find in Old Navy or Abercrombie. You get the sense that she's scouring the internet and going on fashion blogs, then picking through vintage clothing stores to put together the perfect outfits.

"Hey, Ms. Tosh," I say, sitting down at one of the computers. "I like your sweater."

"Thanks," she says. "Okay, so here are the Scantrons." She points to the big pile of forms that everyone filled out in homeroom today. "And here's where you scan them." She points to a machine that's hooked up to one of the computers. She picks up one of the forms, and then slides it into the slot.

DANVERS, JOSEPH A it says on the screen.

"So just start feeding them all in!" she says. "It shouldn't take too long. The hard part is going to be running the booth at lunch."

I look at her, aghast. "So the whole thing . . . the whole process is computerized?" How am I supposed to match Blake up with Sam, and myself up with Kevin, if the whole thing is computerized? That's totally going to ruin my plan! I was even thinking about maybe possibly hooking Sophie Burns up with Taylor Meachum, just to drive her crazy.

"Yes," she says, nodding. I must have a scandalized look on my face, because she says, "You didn't think we were going to be going through them one by one, did you?"

"Well, yeah," I say. "I mean, kind of."

"That would take forever!" She laughs. "Now, can I trust you to stay in here by yourself for a little while and get started? I have to run some papers down to the office, and then I have a meeting with Mr. Standish. I'll be back to check on you in a little while."

"Sure." I smile weakly.

Great. Now what? Everything is totally wrecked! Now I won't be able to make sure that Blake gets matched with Sam. In fact, he'll probably end up get- ting matched with Sophie Burns, and then Sophie will start going out with Sam, and Blake will be so upset that she'll want to move back in with her mom, and I'll have no soon-to-be sister and no BFF prospect, unless a new kid moves here and I'm able to snag her before someone else does.

Although . . . Thinking about it, I'm not sure why I even care. I mean, let's face it. Blake hasn't exactly been the friendliest or nicest person to me. She made me ask for and get dogs that I didn't even want, and then when it came time to take care of them, she kind of disappeared. Not to mention that she tried to con me into tricking my mom and Will into having a boy/girl party. At our house! Boys! At our house! I mean, who knows what kinds of things she might expect to go on there? What if she wants to play Spin the Bottle or Seven Minutes in Heaven? What if there's slow dancing and no one wants to dance with me? She's kind of put me in some horrible positions, when you really think about it, and so if she can't get matched up with who she wants, then, honestly, that's just—

Wait a minute. There's a manual override. On the screen. A manual override option. Which means you can go in and enter WHATEVER YOU WANT. It must be if the machine messes up, like for teachers who are using the Scantrons for tests, if they mess up with an

answer or if the pencil mark isn't dark enough or whatever. So all I have to do is find Blake's answer sheet, and
then when it goes through the machine, give it a manual override. Then I can enter Sam's name, so that it
comes out all printed on a page, ready for her to receive
at lunch.

Of course, then I have to do the same thing with
Sam's, and I'd also have to find who really got matched
up with Sam and then give them whoever really got
matched up with Blake. And if I want to do mine, too,
I'll have to do the whole process over. Which could get
kind of complicated, and I'm not sure I have time before
Ms. Tosh gets back. Which is why I should get started.

I'm up from my chair and pawing through the big
stack of papers, looking for the ones that say Sam
Humphrey and Blake Scalabrini. I hope they haven't
already gone through the machine, although I didn't
notice them, and if they had I guess I could just—

"Hey!" a voice yells from the door, and I scream and
drop all the papers I'm holding. They cascade down to
the floor in a storm of Scantrons.

"Wow," Sam says, walking into the room and grinning
at me. "I guess you were really focused on the task, huh?"

"No!" I say. "I mean, yes, I was focused on the task.
It's . . . important that I get everything done correctly."

"It's a matchmaking service," he says. "It's not rocket science." Then he sits down next to me. Very much next to me. As in, very close to me. It's kind of making me uncomfortable, if you want to know the truth. And not in a bad way. More in a making my stomach go all floopy kind of way.

"If you're looking for Ms. Tosh," I tell him, "she had a meeting in the principal's office."

"Is she in trouble?"

"No, she just—"

"That was a joke."

"Oh." Right. A joke. Obviously my nerves are a little fried since Sam almost caught me messing with the results of the questionnaire. Not that I was doing anything really that wrong. I mean, he even said himself, it isn't rocket science.

"So how's Gus?"

"Gus?"

"Yeah, your dog, Gus?" He reaches over and picks up a Scantron from the stack and then sticks it in the machine.

"What are you doing?" I ask.

"What does it look like I'm doing? I'm feeding the paper into the machine."

"Yeah, but . . . that's my job."

"And my job is to help you."

"But I don't need any help."

"I don't mind."

"Um . . ." I rack my brain, trying to figure out a way to get him out of here. But I have no clue. If it were Blake, I could just tell her that Sam was looking for her. Preferably somewhere far away, like on the other side of the school. But, obviously, that's not going to work here. I wonder what Sam's into. Dogs, obviously. But I can't just say there's a dog looking for him on the other side of the school—he's not that stupid. In fact, he's actually not stupid at all. I remember he always got good grades, one time he even beat me on a science test. Which doesn't usually happen, since science has always come super easy to me, it's like my best subject. Of course, not this year, since our teacher is pretty clueless, he's always—

"What did you put for number one?" Sam's asking.

"Number one on what?"

"The matchmaking questionnaire."

"Those answers are confidential, thank you very much."

He rolls his eyes. "It's not like they're asking you something superpersonal."

I pull the Scantron he's holding out of his hand and look at him. "Did you hear about the dog that's loose on the other side of school?" Desperate times call for desperate measures.

"The what?" He frowns.

Then, suddenly, like an angel from above, Hayden Frye sticks his head into the room. "Yo, Humphrey," he says. "We gotta get to lunch. Brendan's going to try to eat a whole pizza and then keep himself from puking it all up."

"Gross," Sam says. But he's grinning. "Catch you later, Avery." He pulls a strand of my hair as he passes by, and a weird little butterfly shoots all around in my stomach.

I decide to ignore it. I glance at the clock. Great. I only have, like, ten more minutes. I start flipping through the Scantrons at a horribly fast pace, trying to find the ones I need—mine, Blake's, Sam's, whoever got matched with Sam. . . . God, this is going to be complicated.

In the end, I have to wait until all the Scantrons have gone through, then take each paper that I need, refeed it into the machine, and manually override everything and type in everyone's matches. I'm sure there's a better, easier way to do it, but I couldn't figure it out. How annoying. I barely make it before Ms. Tosh gets back.

"How's it going?" she asks.

"Great!"

"Are you sure?" she asks. "You look a little . . . flustered." She's looking at me like she's really concerned.

"Fine!" I squeak. "I, um, better get to fourth period. It's going to be a busy lunch!"

I gather up my books and run out of there before I say something that could totally blow my cover. Yikesss.

seven

"WATCH OUT!" JESS YELLS AS SOMEONE almost knocks the table over. It's lunchtime, and Rina, Jess, and I are manning the student council booth. And people are, like, totally freaking out trying to get their matches. You'd think that in these trying economic times people wouldn't have five dollars to spend on getting their matches, but noooo. People can't wait. One girl even offered Rina twenty dollars to cut the line. Rina said no, of course. I was torn. I kind of wanted her to say yes, since it would mean more money for the children's hospital. Of course, then we'd have to start worrying that other people would start offering more money to cut the line, and then it really would be chaos. Not to mention it would seem like we were taking bribes, which really isn't good in any form of government.

Anyway, then the girl, this eighth grader who had ridiculously shiny hair, offered to give Rina a free make-over along with the twenty dollars, and that clinched it that the answer was no. Because let's face it, it would have been fun to have the makeover, but the girl was basically implying that Rina needed one, which wasn't really that cool. So in the end Rina's pride won out over her desire for a semiprofessional makeup job.

"Back up, back up!" Jess yells again.

Someone throws a five-dollar bill down at me and then starts rifling through the box with all the results, grabs theirs out, and runs away.

"Hey!" I shout. "Get back here with that!"

He's gone already, though. Geez. You'd think the boys wouldn't care so much about this whole thing. I knew the girls would be going crazy, and for the most part, they're definitely being crazier (which I've actually noticed about a lot of things—that girls get more crazy, I mean), but the boys are kind of getting into it too. I guess they're nervous about who they're going to get paired up with.

I feel like screaming at all of them that it doesn't really even matter, that this is just some silly little middle-school project. But of course they wouldn't listen.

"No shoving!" Rina calls.

Finally I have to stand up on a chair. "Listen!" I yell. "Everyone better just calm down and quiet down or we've been told to pack up and not start again until tomorrow." This is kind of a lie. Well, totally a lie. We haven't been told that, but it works. A hush goes through the crowd, and they all get organized and fall into line.

I sit back down.

"Good job," Rina says.

"Thanks. Next?"

"Hey!" Blake's at the front of the line. "Isn't this crazy?"

"Sooo crazy," I say. She pulls something out of her bag and shows it to me. It's an invitation. *Blake and Avery's Last-Minute Leap!* it says. *Cancel your plans and come party with us this weekend!*

"I thought this was supposed to be your birthday party," I say. "Why does it say Blake and Avery are having a party?"

"Because you're throwing it too," she says. "I couldn't just have a birthday party for myself as soon as I got here. People would think I was totally stuck-up. Plus no one has birthday parties anymore, that's lame."

I want to point out that she was the one who said she was having a birthday party in the first place, that that's how we were even allowed to *have* the party, but something tells me that definitely wouldn't go over too well.

"So, ah, now we're just having a party? Like, for no reason?"

"Officially, yes," she says. "Unofficially, you're throwing it for me to welcome me to my new school, so if anyone asks, say that. Also, the theme is 'cancel your plans.' Like it's so fab that even though it's last-minute, you have to come. Get it?"

"Got it," I say, even though I kind of don't.

"So do you have my match?" she says. "I really cannot wait to see who I got."

"Me neither," I say, wondering if the expectant look I have on my face is expectant enough for her to believe that I have no idea. I hand her the envelope, and she rips open the paper, then gets a confused look on her face.

"So who is it?" I ask. Why does she look confused? I guess maybe because she never in her wildest dreams thought she'd get matched with Sam. I mean, let's face it, they didn't exactly hit it off so well the other day when she came over to his house. It wasn't horrible or anything, but I wouldn't have called them soul mates. He got along better with me than he did with her. Not that me and Sam are soul mates, and not that it even matters because no one is soul mates. This whole exercise is totally pointless, with a whole matchmaking thing that is less effective than those internet dating sites that promise you total compatibility.

"Kevin Hudson," Blake says. She's frowning down at the paper. "I have no idea who that is." She looks around, like maybe I'm going to point him out, but now I'm the one who's confused.

"Kevin Hudson?" I ask. "That's impossible." I rip the card out of her hand and double-check that her name is on the front, and that Kevin Hudson is written inside.

"Why is it impossible?" She frowns, and then looks up at me with horror in her blue eyes. "He's not the one who makes burp noises with his armpit at the back of the cafeteria, is he?"

"No," I say. "That's Taylor Meachum." Taylor Meachum, who I hooked up with Sophie. I figured as long as I was at it, I might as well have some fun.

"Oh, thank God. So then why is it impossible? Is this Kevin kid completely horrible?"

"No, it's just . . ." I'm not even really listening to her, and I'm totally not paying attention to the girls behind her in line who are starting to complain that everything is taking too long. Thumb, thumb, thumb. I thumb through the box, looking for my name. Avery LaDuke. I rip open the envelope.

"Ooh," Blake says, watching me. "I get it. You like

Kevin. Don't worry, Avery, I'm not going to go after him or anything. I like Sam, you know that."

Oh no, oh no, oh no. How, how, how could this have happened? Seriously, how could I have been so stupid? I checked and double-checked, didn't I? Actually, no, I never double-checked. I was rushing so I wouldn't get caught. And besides, it wasn't a task you needed to double-check, it was so easy, except apparently it wasn't. Somehow I mixed up the matches. I thumb through the box again and open Sophie's paper. "Taylor Meachum," it says. Well, at least I didn't screw that one up.

"Who did you get matched with?" Blake's asking. And then she reaches over and grabs the card I'm holding out of my hand. Her eyes narrow. And then she frowns as she reads the name: "Sam Humphrey."

"Now, girls," my mom says as we pull up in front of the Harbor Point Restaurant after school. "Make sure you're honest with me. You're not going to hurt my feelings if you don't like the food, we need to make sure that everything is perfect."

"Don't worry," Blake says. "We'll be honest, won't we Avery?"

It's after school, and we're going to a tasting at the Harbor Point Restaurant to test out food for my mom's wedding. Apparently we're going to taste a bunch of stuff, and then decide what we like. I thought we should just have a buffet, but my mom thinks buffets at weddings are tacky. I don't understand why. Everyone likes buffets. You can have as much as you want of whatever you want. Everyone goes away happy. I hope she at least lets me pick some of the music. I'm a pretty good DJ, if I do say so myself.

"We'll be honest," I say, giving Blake a smile. Luckily, Blake wasn't mad about me getting hooked up with Sam, because she "knows it's just a silly student council project." (Of course, I'm pretty sure that if *she'd* gotten matched up with Sam, she wouldn't have thought it was so silly, but whatever.)

So anyway. All's well that end's well. Although it hasn't really totally ended, since everyone at school is asking everyone who they got matched with. But it's not like anyone is actually going to do anything about it. Like, it's not like I'm going to ask Sam out, and it's not like Blake is going to ask Kevin out. And Sophie definitely isn't going to ask Taylor Meachum out, although I heard that he's been following her around all day.

"Hellllooo!" I look up to see a woman, about sixty or so, twirling into the dining room of the Harbor Point. Seriously, she's twirling. She's wearing a long black dress with flowing sleeves, a pair of black tights, and high black shoes. "You must be Sarah!" She kisses my mother on both cheeks and says, "I'm Angeline. I am your caterer!"

I'm pretty sure my mom hasn't totally decided on who's going to be her caterer yet (hence the tasting of all the food) so this lady is totally jumping the gun.

"Oh, um, hello," my mom says. She seems a little ruffled by Angeline's enthusiasm, but if you didn't know her as well as I do, you wouldn't be able to tell. "This is my daughter, Avery, and my soon-to-be stepdaughter, Blake."

"Such gorgeous girls!" Angeline raves. "You, with the hair! And you, with the skin!"

I don't know whose hair and whose skin she's talking about, but either one is fine with me, really, so I just smile and Blake does the same.

"You do not look old enough to have teenage children," Angeline says. She reaches into her bra and pulls out a cigarette, not lit, and then starts sucking on the top of it. "But you don't look old enough to be divorced, either. Me and my Homer, we've been together forty-two years this May."

"Wow," my mom says.

"Wow," Blake says.

"Wow," I say, mostly because I don't want to be left

out. I don't really think being with someone for forty-two years is really all that impressive. I know tons of people who've stayed together for a long time when they should have broken up. Take Sophie's parents, for example. Her parents sleep in separate rooms and her dad is always away on business trips. They should have ended it ages ago.

Angeline leads us over to a round table that's mosaicked in Tuscan tiles, and plops us down into velvet chairs. "I hope you girls brought your appetites."

"I did," Blake says. "But I don't want to eat too much. I need to buy a new dress for my party, and I don't want to look like a heifer."

Angeline looks like maybe she's been slapped. "Girls, girls, girls! Curves are beautiful! I will fatten you two up in no time."

She disappears into the back, and as the door to the kitchen opens, the most amazing smells of garlic and tomatoes and something else warm and spicy come wafting out. My mouth waters. I'm definitely not worried about looking like a heifer at the party, so I say bring it on.

Three hours later, we're all stuffed to the gills. We've eaten appetizers (calamari, mozzarella bread, and fried zucchini dipped in tomato sauce), entrees (chicken marsala, filet mignon, roasted red pepper ziti, and chicken and broccoli alfredo), and desserts (tiramisu and Italian mascarpone cheesecake.)

"Oooh," Blake says, as we walk to the car. "I'm going to have to spend, like, three hours in the gym to work all that off."

"You're so skinny," I say. "A little bit of food isn't going to hurt you."

"So what did you think?" my mom asks as she unlocks the doors to our van.

"Loved it," Blake says. "Except for the fact that I'm going to have to be rolled home."

"Me too," I say. "But Angeline, what was up with her?"

"Yeah, she's definitely a little bit cuckoo," Blake says.

"You've never met Angeline, Avery?" my mom asks. She glances at me in the rearview mirror.

"No," I say. "Why would I?"

"She lives around the corner from us," my mom says. "That's how I know her. She brought us that delicious zucchini bread a few weeks ago."

I vaguely remember something about zucchini bread being brought to our house, and my mom making some kind of really big fuss about it, but once I heard that vegetables were in bread, I decided I wasn't interested.

I rest my head against the window and lapse into a food coma as we pull around the corner.

"See?" my mom says. "There's her house."

"That's her house?" I say at the same time that Blake says, "That's her house?"

I turn around and we look at each other. "Angeline is Sam's grandma!" we say at the same time. And then we burst into giggles. I vaguely remember my mom mentioning something about Sam's grandmother being a caterer, but I totally forgot!

"Speaking of Sam, how's the birthday party planning coming?"

"Good," Blake says quickly. She turns around and looks at me. "Right, Avery?"

"Right," I say, figuring out that her tone means she probably doesn't want to mention that it's morphed from a birthday party into something called a "Last-Minute Leap."

"Wanna take Princess and Gus for a walk?" Blake asks me as we pull into our driveway. "We can walk off some of the food we just ate."

"Sure," I say. "I'm going to get a glass of water and grab a sweatshirt, and then I'll meet you out front with Gus in five?"

"See ya there," she says. She heads toward the garage

to grab Princess's leash, and I guzzle a glass of water from the kitchen, then run upstairs to my room. I slip into my baby blue hoodie, the one with the silver star on the back that's been washed so many times that it's super soft and warm, then start the process of getting Gus ready for his walk.

You'd think it would be easy, that I could just snap his leash on him and go, right? Wrong. Gus gets so excited to go outside that you have to show him the leash slowly, then slip it on him slowly, then walk him outside slowly, even if he's yanking. Otherwise he'll just go full steam ahead, and you'll end up on the ground or with your arm practically coming out of its socket. Worse, Gus will sometimes get so excited he'll jump onto the door and try to gouge holes in it with his nails, or maybe have an accident in the front hallway, which I then have to clean up.

"Gus?" I swear I say it, like, only a touch above a whisper, but he comes rushing own the hall toward me, then jumps up, practically knocking me over. "Oh, Gus," I say. I can't be mad at him. He's so happy to see me that I have to be nice. I mean, he loves me. It's not my fault he gets so excited.

I clip his leash on and try to walk him slowly toward the door, but he's pulling me along so fast I can hardly keep up. Finally I get him out on the porch, and when I do, I stop short.

There, on the front lawn, is Sam Humphrey. He's got on these khaki pants and really white sneakers that look almost brand-new, and the late-day sun is glinting off his hair, and he's walking across the lawn, and for a second my stomach is flipping oh so fast, the same way it did in the computer lab earlier, which is crazy because I don't like him, Blake likes him. And besides, he's Sam Humphrey, and then Gus is leaping toward him and my feet start going, going, going, and I can't stop myself, and the next thing I know, Gus is leaping up and onto Sam.

"Hey, boy," Sam says, super calm like he's the Dog Whisperer or something. "Down."

Gus sits down immediately. Sam reaches down and scratches behind Gus's ears. Gus just sits there, grinning like he's the luckiest dog on earth. Which I guess he kind of is. I mean, he's practically running my life.

"Um, where's Blake?" I ask, looking around.

"I don't know," he says.

"Weren't you coming over to find her?"

"To find Blake?"

"Yeah."

"Why would I come over to find Blake?"

"Because . . ." Something tells me that *Because she likes you and therefore you should like her back and you guys were flirting that day on the bus and so you should want to come over to say hi to her* isn't going to cut it. "We saw your grandmother today," I blurt.

"And she was talking to Blake?" Sam blinks, looking confused.

"Um, no, she . . . We were at her restaurant. Our parents are getting married. Not our parents, mine and yours, our parents mine and Blake's. But you know that already. Anyway, the food was really good. I like calamari a lot." I'm babbling like a complete and total crazy person.

"Yeah, my gram's a really good cook," Sam says. "She's owned the Harbor Point forever."

"That must be cool," I say. "Your grandparents owning a restaurant." I look over my shoulder anxiously for Blake. For some reason, being alone with Sam is making me nervous, like something's coming that I might not be ready to deal with.

"Yeah, it is." He looks down at the ground, and for a second, he looks nervous too. So nervous that I'm sure, I'm positive, he's going to blurt out something completely embarrassing and totally secret, which just *has* to be the fact that he likes Blake. So when he says, "Did you know that we got matched up today by the match-making service?" I'm totally thrown.

Okay. Don't panic. Just pretend that it's no big deal. Sam is a very rational person. He is not going to be thinking about some kind of matchmaking project as something that should be taken seriously.

"Um, well . . . I mean, I didn't exactly look at my paper. I mean, I did look at it, but it . . . it was blurry."

Sam is looking at me like I'm nuts. "What was?"

"What was what?"

"Blurry."

"My paper. Um, my match. It was blurry, I couldn't read it."

"So you didn't know that I was your match?"

"Nope." I grin. "Well, now I know. How funny! Especially since you like paintball, and I put that I like to stay home and watch movies."

"I put that I like to stay home and watch movies," Sam says.

"You did?"

"Yeah. Paintball's cool, but sometimes you just need to stay in and chill, you know?"

"Yeah."

"So about this party you're having—"

"Oh!" I cut him off because I'm so totally happy that

he's talking about something other than the fact that we're matched up. "Yeah, it's pretty awesome, isn't it? It's an unofficial welcome party for Blake." Gus is sniffing around a flower that has, like, the one bee that hasn't gone into hibernation or whatever bees do in the fall buzzing around it, and I shoo him away so that he doesn't get stung. Poor Gus. He's so trusting that he doesn't even get that bees are out to sting him.

"That's cool," Sam says. "So are we supposed to bring dates? To your party?"

"Yes!" I shriek. "Dates are totally allowed!" Of course, my mom and Will definitely didn't say anything about bringing dates, but they don't really need to know who's with who, now do they? I mean, if people want to bring dates, that should be their business. If Sam wants to ask Blake, that should totally be allowed. And it's not like it's going behind my mom and Will's back, since really, they're the ones who said we could have the party. And that we could invite boys. So all the dates would be there already. Although I guess technically someone could try and bring a date who wasn't invited, but then we could just—

"So do you want to go with me?" Sam asks.

My mouth flops open. "What?"

"Do you want to go with me? To Blake's party?"

"Like, be your date?"

"Yeah," he says, grinning. "That's what we were just talking about. Are you okay, Avery?" He kneels down and looks at Gus. "Avery didn't fall and hit her head today, did she, boy?" Gus looks up at him with this look on his face like, *Heck if I know, buddy, she always seems crazy to me.*

"But why?"

"Why do I want to go on a date with you?"

"Yeah," I say.

"Because we got matched up together," he says.

"So?"

"So? That has to mean something, right?" He winks at me.

"No!" I say, throwing my hands up in the air. Gus takes that as his cue to start wandering, and in about five seconds flat, he has me all tangled up in his leash.

"No, it doesn't mean anything?"

"Of course it doesn't mean anything!" What is wrong with him, anyway? I thought he was supposed to be smart. "What is wrong with you, anyway? I thought you were supposed to be smart."

"I am smart," he says. "I'm a grade ahead in math."

"Well, I guess they mean what they say when they say that people who have book smarts are usually lacking in common sense." Except for me, of course. I have great book smarts, and I'm very good when it comes to common sense.

"You think *I'm* lacking in common sense?"

"Yes," I say. "Why are you repeating everything I'm saying?" He really shouldn't be doing that. I'm getting dizzy enough with Gus spinning me all around. "Gus! Bad dog! Stop!"

"Dogs don't respond to negative reinforcement," Sam says. He reaches down and grabs the leash, then slowly starts pulling Gus all around me, untangling him as he goes. "Good dog, Gus," Sam instructs, and Gus sits there patiently. Sam pulls a dog biscuit out of his pocket and gives it to Gus, who chews it daintily and then stares back up at Sam with adoration. God. First it's, like, every girl at my school, and now even my *dog's* in love with Sam Humphrey. Seriously, it's gotta be the hair. It has magical powers or something, I swear.

"So, the party? Are we going or not?"

"Not."

"Why?"

I sigh. "Are you telling me that you really believe in that ridiculous matchmaking service?"

"No," he says. "I don't believe it's going to tell me who I'm going to marry." He grins. "But it's cool to at least have fun with it, right? And I think you're cool and fun and cute and interesting, and I want to get to know you better. Come on, Derrick Fisher's going with Tia Marrone, his match."

"Oh, well, if Derrick Fisher's doing it . . ." I roll my eyes, but my lips are sliding up on the sides into a smile. Wait a minute. Am I . . . I'm not . . . this isn't flirting, is it? I don't think so. Flirting definitely involves, like, hair-twirling and calling a guy some kind of weird pet name, and then pulling out your lip gloss and putting it on all slow so that he knows your lips are totally kissable. So this definitely isn't flirting. But it's definitely something. It's borderline flirting, maybe.

Ohmigod. Sam. Has. Asked. Me. On. A. Date. A date! My first date! I've never been asked on a date before. I've never even gone to a school dance before. Well, I have gone, if you count the end-of-the-year sixth-grade dance last year, which I totally don't, since I did nothing but stand near the walls and look kind of lost.

"Hello?" Sam's saying. "Earth to Avery!"

"Sorry." I shake my head and try to clear my mind from all the racing thoughts.

"So do you want to go to the party with me?"

"I told you, no." The words are out of my mouth before I can stop them, and once they are, I realize they're a lie.

A big, fat, huge lie. Because I *do* want to go to the party with Sam, which really makes no sense, because why would I? I don't like him. Do I? God, I must be going crazy. I'm overworked, probably. It happens to grown-ups all the time. They get overworked and then they start doing crazy things. Probably getting a dog was what pushed me over the edge.

"Why not?" Sam asks, but he doesn't sound mad. He sounds more amused, like maybe he knows that I really do want to go with him.

"I just—"

"Hey, guys!" Blake says, coming bouncing out of the house. She's wearing a new flippy skirt that she didn't have on just a few minutes ago.

"Why'd you change?" I ask, suddenly a little annoyed. "And where's Princess? I thought we were going to—"

She elbows me in the side, and I clamp my mouth shut.

"So what are you guys talking about?"

"Nothing," I say quickly.

"We were talking about the party you guys are having," Sam says.

"Blake!" I almost scream, pulling on her arm. "Isn't that Princess?" I point toward the window, where Princess is looking out at us, her paws up on the ledge. "I think she wants to come out here."

"Would you mind walking them?" Blake asks. "I want to ask Sam about something we were talking about the other day."

She grabs Sam's arm and pulls him away down the street. What? Why? Why would she just leave me here, all alone in the yard? Oh. Right. Because she wants to be alone with him. But then why would Sam leave me here, all alone, after he just asked me to the party?

"Whatever," I say to Gus as I watch them mosey on down the street, Blake talking a mile a minute. "I don't even like him anyway. His hair is way too shiny." And then I go inside to get Princess.

eight

REASONS I HAVE DECIDED I AM DONE
being nice to Blake:

1. She made me get a dog that I don't even like. (Fine,
   he's growing on me. But that doesn't change the
   fact that I didn't want him in the first place, and
   that she convinced me to get him and then basically left me to walk him *and* her dog, like, 90
   percent of the time.)
2. She obviously doesn't even want to be BSFs
   (Best Sisters Forever). Which doesn't really make
   much sense, since she doesn't have a sister, and
   I've been nothing but nice to her.
3. My room is still not finished being painted, and
   I know it's irrational, but I blame Blake.

4. It's going to be harder to like Sam if Blake is actually being nice to me.

When I wake up early on Saturday morning, it's because
Blake is humming. Some really annoying song that
sounds like all you have to do is listen to it for, like, a
second before it gets stuck in your brain and refuses to
get out.

I shove my head under my pillow, but, unfortunately,
all that does is alert her to the fact that I'm awake.

"Avery?" she sings to the tune of the song. "Are you
awake?"

I lie still and hope she goes away. Instead, she pulls
the covers down off my head and says, "I saw you move!"

"Impossible," I say, grabbing the covers and pulling
them back over my head. "And if you did, I was doing it
in my sleep."

"It was definitely an awake move," she says. She grabs
my arm and pulls me into a sitting position. "Look!" she
says, moving her arms all around with a flourish. "Look,
look, look what I've been doing!"

I peer out blearily into the room. My eyes focus on
the used-to-be-only-half-done-but-now-completely-done
green walls. "You painted?" I ask incredulously.

"Yup!" She twirls all around. "Last night, after you fell

asleep. I kept super, super, super quiet. Doesn't it look amazing?"

"It actually does," I say grudgingly. Who'd have thought that Blake was such a great painter? Although when I think about it, it kind of does make sense. She always has these great nail polish jobs, like with rainbow colors and no smudges.

"And," she says, "I made you pumpkin spice muffins. And a hot chocolate."

She pulls a silver tray off the desk and brings it over to the bed. On it are two delicious-looking muffins, all golden, with white icing on the top, and a little pot that looks kind of like a thermos sitting in the middle. Two mugs are on the tray, along with an orange flower in a vase.

"Where'd you get the flower?" I ask, reaching for a muffin.

"Took it out of Angeline's garden," Blake says. She plops down on the bed and pours herself some hot chocolate.

"You stole it out of her garden?"

"I didn't *steal* it," Blake says. "I picked it." She takes a few marshmallows out of a little dish that's sitting on the tray and drops them into her hot chocolate.

"Yeah, but it wasn't yours."

"They were about to die anyway." Blake shrugs, and I take a bite of muffin.

"Ohmigod," I say. "These are amazing."

"Vanilla pudding mix," she says. "It's my secret ingredient." She bites her lip. "So, listen," she says. "I wanted to say I was sorry for the whole thing with the dogs." She takes a big breath. "I just . . ." She sets her hot chocolate down and turns on the bed so that she's facing me. "It was hard."

"What was hard?"

"Getting a dog. My dad always said no, that I couldn't have one, and then you just asked and your mom said yes like it was nothing and we got them and . . . I don't know, it seemed like everything was changing. Even though I *wanted* a dog, you know?"

I swallow my bite of muffin, feeling bad for her. "I guess I didn't think of that," I say. "I should have realized that it might be hard for you."

"Yeah," she says, looking a little uncomfortable. "Anyway, the point is, I shouldn't have stuck you with all the work." Then she pulls a list out of her pocket. "So should we get started?"

"On what?"

"On our sisters day. First, we're having breakfast at the Striped Kettle."

"But we just had breakfast."

"That was a warm-up," she says. "Then we're getting mani-pedis and our hair done, then we're going to the mall to buy new shirts, then we're going to see a movie, and then we're going to come home and cook dinner for your mom and Will."

I grin. "You planned all that?"

"Well," she says, "we're sisters now. And that's what sisters do."

The day is amazing. I get my first manicure-pedicure ever, and while I thought I might hate it, it turns out that I don't. It's *sooo* relaxing to have your feet and hands massaged, and they put the polish on so it looks perfect and shiny and smooth. Blake and I both get a bright pink called It's All About Me. It's not very fall, but we decide that we don't care and that we're going to go with what we like.

Then I get my hair cut in layers around my face, and we get our makeup done at one of those free places in the mall, pretending that we have, like, tons of money to spend. (We do this by pretending we're rich, and we let the saleslady know by waving around this fake credit card that Blake found in this new purse she bought, and being like, "Dad said we could get anything we want" and not getting too close so that they can't tell it's a fake.)

Then we buy matching shirts at Forever 21, order soft ice-cream cones with sprinkles and big, fat, soft pretzels with tons of mustard, and walk around the mall with them. I'm having such a good time that I forget about Sam and the matchmaking disaster and everything.

We end up back at home, where we cook dinner for our parents, this really good spaghetti carbonara that has lots of pancetta and onions.

Sunday's spent recovering from our busy day, doing our homework in between watching all the *Twilight* movies on DVD, and munching our way through the rest of the muffins that Blake made.

The weekend is basically perfect, and I'm in such a good mood on Monday morning that when I'm walking down the hall before homeroom, and over the loudspeaker come the words, "Avery LaDuke, please report to Ms. Tosh's room, Avery LaDuke to Ms. Tosh's room, thank you." I'm not surprised

She probably wants to thank me for all my hard work on the student council charity project. We're expecting to have raised thousands of dollars, and I can't wait to pitch her my new idea, which is that in a few months, I think we should have, like, a do-over with different questions. Like, to see if people have changed enough to make sure that they're still soul mates. People will totally go for it.

"Hey!" a voice says in my ear as I'm walking toward Ms. Tosh's room. I jump. Sam.

"Hi," I say. Now that everything's going great with me and Blake, I definitely do not want to mess it up. "What is it?"

"That's how you greet me? With, 'What is it?'"

"Sorry." I force a smile on my face and pick up my pace. "What I meant to say is, 'How are you, what's up?'" I scan the halls for Blake, hoping she doesn't see Sam and me walking together. Not that she would think anything was going on between us, since she doesn't know about how he asked me to our party.

"Good," he says. "Where were you all weekend? I came by on Saturday, but no one was home."

"Me and Blake were at the mall," I say. "And our parents were out doing wedding stuff. And why were you coming by my house?"

"To see if you wanted to hang out," he says easily. "How come you didn't invite me to the mall?"

"Blake and I were having a sisters day," I say. He's walking really close to me now, and I can smell his boy smell—soap and laundry detergent and something that kind of smells like burning leaves—and I turn my head away and try to clear my thoughts. God, he is *sooo* cute.

"Nice," he says. "Anyway, I heard you get called over the loudspeaker, so I figured I'd go with you to Ms. Tosh's room, see if you needed any help."

We're at the door of the classroom now, and I'm just about to tell him no thank you, that I don't need any help, and he can just head along on his merry way, thank you very much, when Ms. Tosh sticks her head out of the room.

"Hi, guys!" she says. "Why don't you both come inside?"

Great.

"So," she says as we sit down. "First, let me just say that the matchmaking project has been a complete and total success. We've raised over three thousand dollars for the children's hospital, which is a wonderful legacy to leave!"

"Yes, well, we did a great job with marketing the project," I say, even though we didn't really do that great of a job with marketing. I mean, we put up a few posters, but it was word of mouth that really got things going. But I make a mental note to remember to put that part about it being a "wonderful legacy" on my college apps. That sounds totally impressive.

"You worked hard," she says. "And the students were

so excited about it, which is why what I'm about to say is even more upsetting." She bites her lip.

"Why?" Sam asks. "What's wrong?" I'm about 99 percent sure she's going to bring up the fact that Kimberlee Rollins fell and twisted her ankle while she was in line to get her results. It's so ridiculous, because Kimberlee is, like, constantly getting all these fake injuries. Last year she totally faked falling in the bathroom on some wet floor tiles. It's because her dad is a lawyer, and I'm pretty sure he's always trying to figure out a way to sue the school.

"Well," Ms. Tosh says. "I don't know how to say this, because I know how hard you two worked on the project, but . . ." She sighs, and looks at us over the top of her glasses. "It seems as if someone has messed with the results."

Everything stops. I feel my face start to get as warm as one of Blake's muffins right out of the oven, and another shot of heat starts in my stomach and flies up into my chest. It's like I'm watching a DVD that's been put on pause, only I'm the one in the movie.

"How?" Sam asks. "And why?"

Ms. Tosh pulls a printed-out piece of paper from one of her desk drawers and slides it across the table to us. I'm frozen like a statue, and so when Sam reaches over and picks it up, I let him. He moves his desk closer to mine so that we can both look at the paper.

I take a deep breath and then scoot toward him. "INCIDENT REPORT" is typed across the top in big letters. Incident report?! What?! It wasn't an *incident*, it was just . . . a situation, if you will. "Incident report" makes it sound like a police report, or something that's going to get someone into a lot of trouble.

"I don't know why," Ms. Tosh said. "But someone apparently hacked into the system and did a manual override of the matches." She indicates the paper. "Since usually the system is used for tests, anytime a manual override is used, an incident report is printed out so the teachers can make sure that they're the ones who did it."

"So an incident report is just a standard thing, then?" I ask. "Something that happens all the time?" How could I have been so stupid? I mean, I really should have thought about that. Of course there would be some kind of alert system! But if it's a standard thing that happens all the time . . .

"No," Ms. Tosh says. "It doesn't happen all the time. And it should never have happened for the matchmaking project, since there was no reason for anyone to get in and change the results. Besides, no one had access to that computer."

Except me, I think, but instead I just arrange my features into what I hope is a very innocent look. "So do you know who did it?" I ask. Wow. My voice sounded very squeaky right there. Sam looks at me out of the corner of his eye, and then raises one eyebrow.

"No," Ms. Tosh says. "Right now the system is only able to tell us that a manual override was used, but we won't know what was changed until the IT guys can get into the archives and take a look. Unfortunately, that could take a few days. Apparently finding out who messed up our project is not a high-priority tech request." She looks annoyed at this last part.

"It doesn't really matter," I try. "Since it was just a matchmaking project."

"That's true," Ms. Tosh says. "But we can't have people going around and just changing things like that. It's a breach of security, and it compromises the integrity of our whole project. Avery, did you see anyone around the computer lab while you were there?"

"No," I say. "It was only me."

"I stopped by for a few minutes," Sam says. "And Avery's right. We were the only ones there."

"It's possible that someone accessed it from a remote location." She gives a shake of her head, like she can't believe kids these days and their crazy hacking abilities.

"And if that's the case, I suppose the school will have to launch an investigation."

Yikes. This is starting to sound serious. "Well, honestly, I don't think it's that big of a deal," I say. "In fact, I think that maybe we should just all move on." I give a shrug, like *Well, these things happen and what can you do?* and then I say, "In fact, I was thinking that we should do a bonus project, you know, like a separate matchmaking service. Or we could compile a list of everyone's stories with the project, and put them together in a book, and then sell it."

Ms. Tosh frowns. "I don't think so, Avery," she says. "The last thing we want is for the students to tire of the experiment, since I think we could definitely have a successful repeat of it next year."

Wow. Talk about it not being my day.

"I also," Sam says, "don't think we should move on from this whole changing-the-results thing."

"What do you mean?" I ask.

"I mean," he says, "that if someone is messing around with our projects, then that individual should be brought to justice."

Oh, for the love of . . . Brought to justice? What does he think this is, an episode of *Judge Judy*?

"I really don't think it's that big of a deal," I insist.

"Well, I do," Sam says.

"Well, you're not in charge of the project," I tell him. But it's no use.

Ms. Tosh nods her head and then says, "I agree, Sam. This is really serious and needs to be dealt with, not to mention the fact that if there *is* a security breach in our computer system that can be accessed remotely, we need to figure it out."

She drones on for another couple of minutes, and then writes us both passes back to class. Once we're out in the hall, I whack Sam in the shoulder.

"What was that about?" I ask.

"Ow," he says, rubbing his shoulder. "What was what about?"

"All that detective talk!" I say. "All that talk about how you thought whoever hacked in should be prosecuted to the full extent of the law!"

"I never said that," he says. "I just said that we should—" He stares at me then, and his mouth drops open. "Oh my God!" he says. "You did it! You're the one who messed with the results!"

"That's ridiculous," I tell him. I turn around and start walking down the hall, indicating that, you know, this conversation is over, since I'm obviously totally innocent and don't like it being implied otherwise.

"Wow," he says, running after me. "You are a *really* horrible liar. And wow, I didn't know you had it in you."

"I didn't do it!" I say.

"So wait a minute," he says. "That means we didn't really get matched up. You made yourself get matched up with me!"

Oh, God. "No, I didn't," I say.

"Yes, you did!"

"No," I say. "I—" And then I stop, because I don't know what to say. I can't tell him I did it because of Blake, and that it was a big mistake. Blake would kill me if she knew I told him that. And besides, even if I *did* want to tell him it was because of Blake, I'm not going to admit to Sam Humphrey that I messed with the student council project. He can suspect me all he wants, but he can't prove anything.

Then Mr. Carter, one of the eighth-grade science teachers, pokes his head out of his classroom. "Where are you two supposed to be?" he asks.

"Sorry," I say. "We were just getting back to class."

"Then go," he says, narrowing his eyes at us.

And so we do.

I don't see Sam for the rest of the day, so I have zero opportunities to convince him I wasn't the one who messed up the project. So by the time my mom picks Blake and me up from school so that we can head to our dress fitting, I'm going crazy. So crazy that I don't even have enough mental energy left over to feel upset when the pink dresses are brought out from the back, and Blake and I are marched into separate dressing rooms to try them on.

But when I look in the mirror, I'm surprised to see that I actually don't look that bad. In fact, um, I look kind of amazing. The dress looked good on me before, but now that it's been tailored to fit me specifically, it looks perfect. The fabric falls in soft waves down to the floor, and cinches in at the waist perfectly. And yeah, it's still a little too pink, but it *is* a wedding, and it definitely could be worse (read: petticoats).

When we're done at the dress store, Blake and Will go to the mall to look for new running sneakers, but my mom's tired, and I'm so ready for this day to be over, so my mom and I pick up a pizza and head home. There's a knock on the door just as we're finishing up the last of the crusts, and I go to answer it.

Sam.

"What are you doing here?" I blurt.

"I came to see you."

Gus hears Sam's voice and comes running into the

hallway, his tail wagging. "Hey, boy," Sam says. "You wanna go for a walk?"

Great. Now Gus is getting all riled up, and I can't stop him from freaking out. Which means I'm going to have to take him for a walk or he'll destroy something for sure.

"I'll get the leashes," I say, because I can't bring Gus without bringing Princess, even though she's technically Blake's responsibility. Princess stands there super well-behaved when I clip the leash on her, and then we bring the dogs outside.

"So," I say as we walk. "I think we should talk."

"Me too," Sam says. "Definitely." We keep walking, and even though we both just said we needed to talk, neither one of us says anything. Finally Sam says, "So why don't you want to go to the party with me if you made it so that we'd get matched up?"

I take a deep breath. "I didn't want to match us up," I say. "It was . . . I mean, it was a mistake. That wasn't supposed to happen."

"So you admit that you *did* fix the matches?"

"No," I say. "I didn't. I just . . ." God, I really should have had a plan.

"Oh my God," Sam says suddenly, stopping in the middle of the street. Gus sits down and looks at him, all confused. Sam looks at me, realization dawning on his face. "Blake likes me, and you were trying to match me up with her."

"No, she doesn't," I say, and keep walking with Princess. "And no, I wasn't." God, how is he so smart? Seriously, he might be, like, the most underrated smart person ever. Does everyone even know how smart he is? Or do they just like him because he's cute and confident and a lacrosse star?

"Yes you did, and yes she does," he says. "But it's okay, you don't have to admit it." We walk in silence for a few minutes. The dogs are actually being good for once, walking along beside us.

"But I don't like Blake," he says. "I like you."

I like you, too, I want to say, because there's really no denying it. I like Sam Humphrey. He's funny and sarcastic and smart and caring and he loves dogs and he wants to go to the party with me and I've just realized he has very, very kissable lips and I want to tell him all of that. But instead I just take Gus's leash out of his hand. "I'm sorry," I say. "I . . . I have to go."

nine

WHEN BLAKE GETS HOME THAT NIGHT, I pretend I'm asleep. And when she jumps on my bed Tuesday morning before school, I take a couple of extra minutes to open my eyes.

"Wake up!" she says. "Your mom said you went for a walk with Sam yesterday. He came over to see me?!" She twirls around the room happily.

I don't say anything, but it doesn't matter, because she's over in the corner, pulling clothes out of her dresser. "So we have a lot of work to do on this party," she says, "if we want to be ready by the weekend. I mean, we only have four more days. So I was thinking that after school we can go to the party store and get some decorations and stuff before we go and pick up our bridesmaid dresses."

Right. The bridesmaid dresses, which got some final

tweaks after our fitting yesterday, are going to be picked up after school. I forgot about that. I can't believe we're having a party *and* a wedding within the next two weeks. I groan and shove my head back under the pillow. Not that any of this matters. I'm probably going to get in trouble for fixing the matchmaking results, and then I'm going to get suspended from school, and I won't be able to go to the party because I'll be grounded, for, like, ever, and I probably won't be able to go to the wedding, either, because my parents are going to disown me and then—

"Yay!!!" Blake yells, vaulting across the room and onto my bed. She's so happy that I can't help but smile just a little bit. I mean, it's not her fault my life is a total mess.

But my bump up in mood doesn't last that long, even though I'm able to avoid both Ms. Tosh and Sam all day—there's only one close call, when I have to duck into a classroom to avoid Sam, who's walking down the hall with Hayden Frye—and so by the time I'm at the party store with Blake, I'm pretty cranky.

"What do you think of black and white for the colors?" Blake asks. She holds up a package of black-and-white streamers.

"Black and white what?" I ask, glancing at some pink tiaras that are in the corner. I pick up a glittery wand

and swing it around my head. If my life were a movie, it would turn out that this wand was actually a magic wand, and I would wave it over my head and put some sort of spell on Sam that would make him like Blake. Then I would put a spell on myself not to like him. And then I would put another spell on Ms. Tosh to forget about the whole INCIDENT REPORT debacle. I wave it around just in case and whisper some gibberish words. Nothing happens. I sigh and put the wand back.

"Everything. Streamers, tablecloths, everything. . . . I saw it on an episode of *One Tree Hill* and it looked amazing."

"Sure," I say, shrugging.

"Fine," she says. "The theme is black, white, and silver."

We load up the cart with tons of decorations in black, white, and silver, and then push the cart up to the cash register. But before we can make it there, we run into Sophie Burns.

"Watch it!" she screeches as I almost push the cart right into her. What is up with me always almost running into this girl? I think it's because she takes up so much space. Not that she's big, she's actually really tiny. She just can't fathom the fact that there might be other people around, since she's so focused on herself.

"Sorry," I say. "I guess I didn't see you there." I don't

add that even if I did, I might have pushed the cart into her anyway. That's just the kind of mood I'm in.

"Because you weren't watching where you were going." She rolls her eyes. Then she glances down into our cart. "Oh, cute," she says. "You're buying things at the discount party store for your party."

"And what are you doing here?" I ask.

"Picking up some paper cups," she says. "My parents are being super lame about letting us drink out of the champagne glasses. Last year, like, ten of them broke and there was sparkling cider all over the place."

"Avery!" Blake yells, running up from aisle four. "I found them, I found the silvery glitter streamers!"

"Adorbs!" Sophie says. "You guys are doing black, white, and silver. That's what Jamison Navaro did at his party last year." She flips her highlighted hair over her shoulder. "See ya."

Blake's mouth drops open as she watches Sophie walk out of the store. Then she shuts it. Then she looks down at all the stuff in our cart. And then she leaves our whole basket right there, in the middle of the store, and walks out.

Blake doesn't say a word the whole drive home, which means I'm the one who has to keep up a constant stream of chatter with Will. And it's not easy, let me tell you. After the party store we picked up the dresses, so I tried to talk to him about that, but he doesn't know anything about dresses. Less than me, even. So then I tried asking him about sports, but I didn't even know what was in season, like if it was time for football, baseball, whatever. So finally we just turned on the radio.

Anyway, I think Blake's in some kind of weird shock having to do with the fact that her party color scheme is ruined. Which, honestly, is kind of silly when you think about it. I mean, we'll just pick a new color scheme. How hard can it be? And why do we have to have a color scheme anyway? That just makes everything so much more complicated. We have enough to plan for, not to mention the fact that boys are going to be coming, which is enough mental stress for anyone to have to deal with, without adding decoration scandals on top of it.

But I want to cheer her up, so after dinner, when Blake settles into the living room to watch a DVD, I decide to go upstairs and Google new color schemes. If I can find something really cool, maybe she'll be in a better mood.

"Avery," my mom calls when I'm halfway up the stairs. "Can you bring the dresses upstairs and hang them in your closet, please?"

"Yes," I yell back. I take our bridesmaid dresses from her and bring them up to my closet. Once they're hanging, I pick up the bottom of the plastic that's covering them and run my finger down over the pink lace. When we picked them up, the shop was getting ready to close, so we were instructed to try the dresses on before the wedding and bring them back if they needed any adjustment. At some point my mom's hairdresser is coming over to try out hairstyles, so we're going to try on the dresses then, and get a picture of how everything is going to hang together.

Although . . . it is really pretty. I lift up the plastic covering a little more. I've never had a dress that was made just for me before. I decide to try it on, even though I'm not supposed to. It's not like I'm going to do anything to it. And honestly, waiting until we get our hair done is kind of silly. What if the dress doesn't fit? Shouldn't we know as soon as possible?

Blake comes walking into the room as I'm lifting the dress out of the shiny cellophane it's covered in.

"What are you doing?" she asks.

"Nothing," I say quickly. I try to put the dress back, but instead of it sliding right back on, the clear crinkly paper gets all tangled up in my arms.

"You were trying on your dress!" Blake says, sounding

shocked. "Even though your mom specifically told us not to!"

"No, I wasn't!" Wow. This paper is *really* not going back over the dress. It's like the crinkliest wrapping ever. I hope they didn't put this stuff on my mom's dress. Because she'd never get her dress out. In fact, she'd probably even think it was some kind of sign or something. Okay, she wouldn't. Because she's not superstitious. But some bride somewhere probably is, and this paper is going to be the death of her wedding.

"Yes, you were," Blake says. "I don't care, you don't have to be, like, embarrassed about it." She flops down on her bed.

"I'm not embarrassed about it," I say, even though I totally am.

"I'm not going to tell on you." She sits up and looks at me trying to get the dress wrapped back up. Then she crosses the room. "They *are* really beautiful dresses, aren't they?"

"Yeah," I say, fingering the material lightly.

"We could probably try them on," she says. "Just once, you know, to make sure they fit."

"True," I say, trying to sound nonchalant. "I mean, it's kind of ridiculous that we should have to wait. It could turn out to be a huge disaster."

"Huge," Blake says, nodding. "Your mom would probably thank us, if we did find something wrong. I mean, who knows how long it will take to fix it?"

"Definitely," I say, even though Trudy at the bridal shop said most minor alterations could be done within twenty-four hours.

I'm totally shy about getting undressed in front of Blake, so I take my dress into the bathroom, and she stays in our room. I pull off my jeans and sweater and pull the dress over my head. It falls in a shimmery halo around my waist and down to my legs. Ohmigod. I love it. I've never worn something so absolutely and completely gorgeous. It kind of makes me realize why people might get so into fashion. I rise up on my tiptoes, trying to see how it's going to look with high heels. I can't completely get the whole idea of it, though, and I wonder if my mom would notice if I grabbed a pair of shoes from her closet. You know, just to try on.

"Avery!" Blake yells from across the hall. "Are you coming?"

"Yes!" I open the door and peek out, looking both ways to make sure the coast is clear, then run across the hall. When I get to my room, Blake and I stare at each other.

"We look beautiful," Blake says, her mouth open. "Even more beautiful than the last time we tried them on."

"Completely gorgeous," I say.

"Take a pic of me!" Blake says, handing me her phone. "I want to text it to Sam."

I take her phone out of her hand, my good mood slightly deflating. "Are you sure?" I ask. "What if he says something to his grandma about how you sent him a pic in your dress, and then she mentions it to my mom?"

"Like that's going to happen," Blake says, rolling her eyes.

"Okay." I snap the pic of her, and then hand her back the phone, watching as she texts it to Sam and swallowing around the lump in my throat.

"Now," she says. "It's time to talk party color schemes."

"Shouldn't we take these off first?" I ask, looking down at the dress. "What if we wreck them?"

"We won't," she says. "And besides, we have to break them in."

"Break them in?"

"Yeah, like how they break in shoes and stuff."

"That makes sense," I say nodding. I mean, as pretty as the dresses look, they definitely feel a little stiff. Probably from never being worn before. So if we can just walk around in them a little, make them conform to our bodies, all the better. Then at the wedding they'll probably look even more fabulous.

I sit down on the bed and pull out my laptop. On it I've started making lists for everything having to do with the party. Blake and I spend the next twenty minutes going over everything, and when we're done, I lie back on my bed, closing my eyes. Party planning is actually very exhausting. I can't imagine planning a whole wedding in such a short time.

"I think we should take these off now," I say to Blake.

"Agreed," she says. We stand in front of the full-length mirror on the back of my closet and pose a little bit, getting one last look at ourselves. I put my hand on my hip and pout at the mirror. Really, I should have taken a pic of myself. Not to send to Sam, of course, but just for myself. My heart catches a little in my throat thinking about Sam, so I do my best to push him out of my thoughts.

Gus comes running into the room then, stopping short when he sees us posing.

"Don't tell anyone we're wearing these," Blake tells him. "We could get in a lot of trouble." Gus cocks his head to one side like he's actually listening, and I giggle.

And then Gus decides it's time to play. He grabs the bottom of Blake's dress and starts to pull on it.

"No, Gus!" I say. "Bad dog!" I grab his collar and try to get him to drop the dress, which is actually against everything I've learned from Sam about dogs. When they act bad, you're supposed to just ignore them, since they learn better with positive reinforcement. But I can't just ignore Gus now—he's pulling on Blake's dress! Blake's dress that needs to be ready for the wedding in a week and a half, Blake's dress that was superexpensive, Blake's dress that she's not even supposed to be wearing.

"Blake!" I command. "Don't move, whatever you do, just DO NOT MOVE!"

"Okay," she says, not looking so sure about this plan. But if she moves, the dress is going to rip.

"Here, Gus!" I say. "Nice Gus! Want a treat?" I run over to my desk and look around frantically for something I can give him as a treat. But there's nothing. Why didn't I think to have some emergency treats on hand for situations like this? I should have known that Gus could start acting up anywhere, anytime.

I walk over to him, my fist closed, and try to trick him by pretending I have something in there. "Come get a treat, Gus!" I say. "Come and get a nice treat!"

Gus looks over, intrigued. He sniffs the air around my fist without letting go of Blake's dress, and when he doesn't smell a treat, he figures out it's a trick and pulls harder. And harder.

Riiiiiippp. The bottom of Blake's dress tears, and Gus,

delighted, runs out of the room with a piece of pink shimmery fabric in his mouth. I go to run after him, but I'm so frantic that I'm not really watching where I'm going, and the next thing I know, I trip. And fall into something wet and sticky.

"What the—" Paint. It's paint. I've fallen into a roller tray of paint. A roller tray of paint that is halfway dry and sticky and disgusting. A roller tray of paint that Blake was supposed to clean up after she finished painting our room. A roller tray of paint that is now all over my dress.

Okay. We just need a plan. I'm pretty sure things like this happen all the time. Well, not *exactly* like this. I'm sure people aren't always getting their dresses ripped by their dogs and then falling into paint. But I know that dress disasters do happen. I think there's even a whole show about it on TV or something. It might even be called *Dress Disasters*. We probably just have to call the place we got it and find out what to do.

"Google the phone number," I instruct Blake. "We'll call and ask them what to do if the, uh, merchandise gets damaged." For a second I wonder if we can just pretend we pulled them out of the plastic like that, but there's no way they're going to believe our dresses were allowed to leave the store with doggie slobber and green paint all over them.

"Oh no, oh no, oh no," Blake is saying. It turns out she's actually not that good in a crisis. She's just been standing there for the past two minutes, talking about how sorry she is and saying, "Oh no, oh no, oh no." I didn't even have the heart to yell at her for leaving the paint out on the floor.

"Blake!" I say. "Now!" I rush back to the bathroom, take off the dress, throw on my jeans and T-shirt, then rush back to my room. I'm relieved to see that Blake's at the computer, at least attempting to do something useful. "I'm going to go and get the scrap of fabric from Gus," I say. "You find the phone number and I'll be right back."

But when I find Gus, he's lying on his dog bed in the family room, calmly watching TV with my mom and Will, acting like nothing's happened. He raises his head and looks at me disinterestedly, then goes back to just lying there. There is no sign of any pink, silky fabric scrap, even though I know it must be around here somewhere.

"Oh, hi, Gus," I say. "How are you doing, boy?" He wags his tail a few times but doesn't get up to greet me. Princess is lying on the couch like well, a princess, and she glances up at me regally.

"Are you taking him out?" my mom asks.

"Um, no," I say. From upstairs, I hear a bunch of thumping. Yikes. I wonder what Blake's doing up there. Whatever it is, it can't be good. "I was just, um, coming down to grab a snack."

I glance around a couple of times, but I don't see any cloth or fabric or even a thread, so eventually I have to just turn around and go upstairs.

"I couldn't find it," I say to Blake. She's sitting in front of the computer, looking a little bit panicked. "What was all that banging?"

"I was trying to see if I could get the dress off without ripping it more," she says. She turns around. "But the fabric is all ripped and caught in the zipper."

"What?!" I ask. I spin her around. "How did that even happen?"

"I have no idea," she says. "But I found the number for the place."

"Perfect," I say. I whip out my cell phone and get ready to dial. Then I stop. "Wait a minute," I say. "We probably shouldn't call the place we got the dresses from."

"Why?" Blake asks. "You think we just could Google a solution? Like, fix it ourselves?"

She sounds excited, and I feel sorry for her obvious delusion. "No, I just mean . . . what if they recognize our voices or something? And decide to call my mom?"

"Good point," Blake says, her eyes widening. "They probably would call your mom! There's probably a law about minors calling them or something."

"I think we should just call a different place, like a random wedding dress place. Or a dry cleaner! Dry cleaners are always fixing things like this. They even have signs in the windows about broken zippers and stuff."

"Perfect," Blake says, her hands already flying over the keyboard. "We can get very specific without them even knowing who we are."

"I guess," I say, not sure how specific I really want to get. I mean, what am I supposed to say? That my rescue dog ate my dress? And that while I was trying to get him off my almost-stepsister I fell in some paint? That seems a little *too* specific. Maybe just tell them the gist of it, you know, like an overview. I'm very good with overviews. I'm always getting ninety-eights on my English essay summaries.

"Here we go," Blake says. "Wedding Dress Restoration, Emergency Line."

"Exactly what we need," I say, copying the number from the screen into my phone. "This is def an emergency."

"Hello, Wedding Dress Restoration," a posh woman's voice says through the line.

"Yes, hello," I say, trying to sound just as posh back. Blake abandons her spot at the computer and comes over, and I put the phone on speaker. "I have a question about some bridesmaid dresses."

"Absolutely, miss," the woman says. "How may I help you?"

"Well," I say. "There is one that is . . . um, torn. Do you guys do any kind of fixing of torn, uh, garments?"

"Yes," she says. "We do."

"What about paint stains?" I ask. "Can you get some paint stains off a dress?"

"It depends on just how bad and how long the paint stains have been on," she says.

"Um, well, it's a light green color, and they've been on for about, um, I dunno, maybe ten or so minutes, as of this phone call."

"We can probably get them off," she says. "Of course, we'd have to see the garment in question."

"Of course," I say.

"Would you like to bring them in?"

I look at Blake. She nods at me.

"Yes, I think I would."

"Fabulous!" she says. "Can you hold for just a moment while I get you a date and a very rough estimate?"

"Yes, thank you very much for your assistance." The

sound of elevator music drifts through the line, and I collapse back onto my pillows. "I think we can get them fixed," I say. "All we have to do is bring them in. How much money do you have?'

"I have, like, fifty dollars of birthday money," she says. "My grandma always sends me a card early."

"I have about twenty-five," I tell her. "Seventy-five should be enough, wouldn't you think?"

"More than enough," she says. "Usually when you go to get things dry-cleaned it's, like, five dollars for a whole suit or something."

I feel the breath I didn't know I was holding rush out of me in one big swoop. Everything's going to be fine. Of course, I don't know how we're going to get the dresses over to this place, which is all the way in Newton, since obviously neither one of us drives. But I'm sure there's a way. If worse comes to worst, we could take a taxi. Yeah, it's not *ideal* (taxis always seem sketchy to me, like the drivers are one step away from kidnapping you—not that I've ever been in a taxi by myself before, although I do watch a lot of those true crime shows on TV), but beggars can't really be choosers, you know? I'm sure it will be fine. Especially since there are two of us. We'll just—

"Hello? Miss?" the woman on the other end of the phone is saying.

"Yes, I'm here." Blake scootches closer to me on the bed so she can hear.

"I did a rough estimate, and for both dresses, it will be three hundred dollars." My mouth drops open.

"I'm sorry," I say. "Did you say three hundred dollars?"

"Yes," she says. "It would have been three hundred and thirty-three dollars, but we're running a special! Ten percent off for all our new customers!" She sounds really proud of herself at that last bit, which is really ridiculous, since no one should be proud of giving someone 10 percent off a rip-off.

"Well," I say, "you should be very disappointed in yourself for trying to take advantage of people. Just because I'm only thirteen doesn't mean I don't know a scam when I see one."

"Yeah," Blake says into the phone. "And don't think we won't be going to the internet with this!"

And then we hang up on her. "We're going to the internet with this?" I ask.

"No," she says. "It's just something that I hear my mom say sometimes when people are messing with her. I guess businesses are really scared of people going to the internet and spreading around how horrible they are."

"Ahh," I say. "Makes sense." I bound back over to the

computer and look at the screen. "So all we need to do is find another place," I say. "So we can find a better price."

I scroll through the names. Best Wedding Alterations. Hmm. I wonder if that's true. That they're the best. Probably not. One time I was watching *The Apprentice*, and Donald Trump said that if you say you're tough, you're not. Which probably means that if you say you're the best, you're actually not. But I don't really care if they're the best, as long as they're the cheapest. Maybe I should try to look for a place called "Adequate and Cheapest Wedding Alterations."

A box pops up on my computer.

HEY——WHATS UP?

It's an IM. From Sam. OMG! It's Sam! Sam is IMing me! I didn't even know he had my IM name! He must have asked someone for it. How cute! I can't believe he's IMing me! I quickly close it out and sign out of instant messenger. I turn around to see if Blake noticed, but she's still just sitting on the bed, looking at her dress forlornly.

"I found another one," I say quickly. "Best Wedding Alterations. Let's call them and find out what kind of better price there is."

But seven calls later, we're still in the same boat. And

by same boat, I mean that we're totally in trouble. I guess it's pretty expensive to get your bridesmaid dresses fixed when you've spilled paint on it and/or ripped it. And it's doubly expensive to get two of them done. It's really a complete and total joke, this whole wedding industry. I mean, they prey on people's emotions and basically can charge them anything they want.

"What are we going to do?" Blake asks. After that last call, where we offered the man who answered seventy-five dollars to do both dresses, and he laughed and hung up on us, Blake has been very upset. At least we were able to get her out of her dress without ripping it any more. Not that it's much of a bright side, since it's still totally unwearable.

"I'm not sure," I say. "Maybe we could—"

The sound of my mom's footsteps comes echoing up the stairs. "Quick!" Blake screams. "Grab the dresses and shove them in the closet!"

Great. Now on top of everything else, we're going to have to get the dresses ironed. Although maybe they dry-clean them once you get them fixed up somewhere. It's the least they can do for all that money, you'd think, right? But maybe not. Those dress people are kind of snotty. One woman thought I was joking when I asked if there was any kind of two-for-one deal, or if they offered coupons. What's wrong with coupons?

"Girls?" my mom asks, knocking on the door to our room. "Are you in here?"

"Yes!" I say. I reach behind my head and grab a book off the shelf, and then throw one at Blake. It bounces off her elbow and lands on her bed.

"Ouch," she says, rubbing her arm. "That really hurt." But I'm in no mood. A little scratch on her elbow is nothing compared to the trouble we're about to be in.

"We're just reading some books," I say as the door opens softly and my mom peeks her head in.

"Oh," she says. She sounds startled. "I was wondering why it was so quiet up here. But then I thought I heard you two on the phone." She looks slightly suspicious, but really, she can't say anything, because like I said, I'm kind of the perfect daughter.

"Nope, we must have just been discussing our books," Blake says.

"What are you reading?" my mom says.

"Um . . ." I look at the book I'm reading. "*Initiation*, the new Canterwood Crest book."

"And I'm reading . . ." Blake looks at the cover of hers. "*All-New Baseball Cards and What They're Worth, 1997 Edition.*"

My mom raises her eyebrows. "It's my dad's," Blake

says, recovering quickly. "He used to be super into baseball cards, and he kind of got me into them too."

"Oh," my mom says, nodding. "Well, don't stay up too late."

"We won't," we say.

My mom shuts the door, and for a second, there's just stunned silence. I look at Blake. Blake looks at me. And then we burst into giggles.

"Now you're into baseball cards?" I ask.

"Oh, yeah, I love them," she says, rolling her eyes. "And honestly, the funniest part? Is that my dad isn't even into baseball cards. I think this is an old book of my grandpa's that somehow got mixed up with some of our stuff that was in the basement."

We don't stop giggling for a long time.

ten

ON FRIDAY, BLAKE STARTS TO HAND OUT the invitations to our Last-Minute Leap. Even though a lot of people already know about it, we decided not to give out any formal invites until today, so that we can keep with the last-minute theme. Blake's super excited, but I can't even *think* about the party with everything else going on. I've spent, like, every spare minute I have trying to figure out how to get the dresses fixed, to no avail. It's enough to give me an ulcer. Not to mention that after a week of not hearing anything about the match-making project and the "incident report" that was going to be investigated, I'm starting to really freak out. I'm kind of hoping that the whole thing was just forgotten about. That happens, right? Cases just get overlooked, due to bureaucratic mismanagement and understaffing.

Anyway, I've been on pins and needles all week, and Blake says a party is just what I need to relax. Easy for her to say. She has no idea that my whole academic future is about to be ruined, not to mention my relationship with my mom.

"This party is tomorrow," Rina says, looking doubtfully at the invitation after Blake hands it to her.

"I know," Blake says. "That's the point. It's like a 'drop your plans' party, because it's going to be so awesome."

Jess looks at her skeptically, so I add, "Seriously, there's going to be a fruit sculpture and everything." There really is, it's not a lie. I'm making it myself. I looked up the directions on the internet, and you, like, make it in a watermelon bowl. It's kind of tricky, but I think I can handle it. Of course, I've never made a fruit sculpture before, but how hard can it be? It's just fruit. No cooking involved, even.

"There might even be Spin the Bottle," Blake says. Rina's mouth drops open. "Bye!" Blake says, then takes off down the hall.

"Is there really going to be Spin the Bottle?" Jess asks. She sounds worried.

"No, of course not," I say. "My parents would never allow that." The bell rings then, and we all head to third period. Of course, our parents would never allow us to have a boy/girl party before either. But I put that out of my head.

"So what's up with Gus?" Sam asks me later at my locker.

"What do you mean?" I glance around the hall to make sure Blake isn't watching.

"I just figured that since you haven't been answering my IMs or texts, and you've obviously been avoiding me at school, you must have been really busy training Gus. Next time I see him, I'll expect him to be able to bring my slippers."

"Gus," I say, "is not doing so well with his training. And that is an understatement." I'm combing through my bag, looking for my purple highlighter. It's the only highlighter I like to write with in science, because it's my hardest subject, and it helps when my notes are in a color that I like to read. I know it sounds kind of silly, but I figure anything that can make me feel the teensiest bit better is totally deserved.

"Uh-oh," Sam says. "That doesn't sound so good. It sounds like something bad happened."

I nod. "Something bad did happen."

"Like what kind of bad?"

"Like the kind of bad that costs you three hundred dollars." Saying the words out loud makes my stomach clench, and I have a vision of my mom's face contorting in horror when she sees the ruined dresses.

Sam's eyes widen. "Ouch," he says. "What did he do?"

I can't tell him, because Blake and I promised each other that we'd keep it a secret, at least until we figure out what to do. It's not like Sam would tell anyone, but what if it slipped out? Like, what if he told his grandmother, and then his grandmother was getting my mom's food ready or something and then she was all, "I heard about that horrible disaster of a daughter and a soon-to-be stepdaughter that you have. Wow, I can't believe they caused hundreds of dollars of damage to their dresses when you're already probably going broke from the cost of this wedding."

"Come on," he says. "Tell me."

I open my mouth, about to tell him what's going on, because I'm going so crazy that I figure talking about it can only help. But the bell rings before I can answer him, so I just say, "It's nothing. I have it under control."

"You sure?" he says.

"Yeah," I say, "I'm sure."

"All right," he says. "I'll text you later." He grins and then takes off down the hall, leaving me staring after him.

And he does. Text me, I mean. Later that night. HEY WHATS UP? WANT 2 TALK ABOUT WHAT GUS DID THAT HAS U SO UPSET?

Obviously it's just a ploy to get me to text him back. Which I'm not going to do. But my stomach is all flippy, and I keep looking at the text, reading it over and over. It's the last thing I look at before I go to bed on Friday night, and the first thing I look at when I wake up on Saturday morning. At one point on Saturday afternoon, I totally weaken and type a text back to him, but then quickly delete it before it gets sent.

It's not just that he texted me that's making me all sparkly. It's that he's concerned about how I feel. I mean, how cute is that?

"This is going to be the best night ever," Blake says on Saturday night, when we're in the kitchen getting ready for the party. And when I say "getting ready," I mean that so far we've basically taken the wrapper off the pepperoni and cheese plate my mom got, and made a playlist on Blake's iPod. Blake kept wanting to put all these slow songs on it, which I didn't think was that good of an idea, but she wouldn't listen to me. We ended up with about a seventy/thirty mix of fast to slow, but if Blake had had her way, it would have been, like, sixty/forty slow. Not that I like fast music either. In fact, I'm kind of a horrible dancer. One time in second grade I tried out for tap, and I didn't make it. And they took, like, everyone.

"Yeah, it's going to be fun," I say, not really meaning it. I'm at the counter, working on my fruit sculpture. Although it's not really a sculpture anymore. It's more like a salad. With lots of grapes, because you don't have to cut those up. Turns out cutting up fruit takes a really long time. Much longer than you'd think. And I'm having trouble focusing due to my distressed mental state.

"Do you need help with that?" Blake asks. She's so excited, she's practically jumping up and down. She's been like that all day, probably because it's her birthday. My mom made her a birthday breakfast of crepes with fresh blueberries and whipped cream, and then Will gave her the gift certificate to Justice that he and my mom got her. And ever since then, she hasn't calmed down, even for one second.

"Yes," I say. "I need help. Bad."

She picks up the internet printout with the directions

on it. "Thirty melon balls." She frowns. "This is going to be a pretty big fruit salad. Do any of your friends even *like* fruit salad?"

"It's a fruit *sculpture*," I hiss, as a melon ball goes flying off the fruit baller I'm holding, sails through the air, hits the ceiling, and then plops onto the floor. "Oops."

"So," Blake says, dropping the directions back onto the counter. "I have a surprise for you." Her eyes are shining with excitement.

"What?" I ask warily. Something tells me it's not that our dresses are totally fixed and waiting upstairs for us, all hung up and dry-cleaned to perfection.

"You'll see," she says.

When I'm finally finished with the fruit sculpture/salad, Blake and I head upstairs to get ready for the party. I stand in front of my closet and pull out my best pair of jeans and a flirty red top that has ruffles on the bottom.

"That's not what you're wearing, is it?" Blake asks.

"Yeah," I say. "Why, what's wrong with it?"

"Nothing, if you're going to your grandma's house."

"Hey," I say. "My grandma is actually very fashion conscious, and she would highly approve of this outfit."

"Well, if she's fashion conscious for an old person, then she probably has no idea what to wear to a Last-Minute Leap where there are going to be boys."

"Probably not," I agree. My grandma really *is* fashion conscious, it's not a lie. But she does still have lace doilies in her kitchen, and she's always wearing things that came from, like, her original 1960s wardrobe. I used to think it was vintage, but I guess maybe it's just . . . old.

"Here." Blake reaches into her closet and pulls out a short silver beaded dress with spaghetti straps. It poofs out at the bottom and has a satiny lining underneath the material of the skirt, which makes it look super shiny. Around the waist is a gorgeous band of shimmery sequins.

"It's amazing," I say, reaching out and fingering the silky material. "But won't I be cold?"

"We'll be inside," she reminds me. "And we're going to be dancing up a storm."

I decide now's definitely not the best time to tell her I'm not going to be dancing. "And here. If you get cold, I have this." She pulls out a long, sheer, deep purple cardigan that ties in the front. So. Cute.

"Ohmigod, I love it," I tell her. I grab her in a hug. "Thank you so much."

We take an hour to get ready, each taking showers, drying our hair, and putting on lip gloss, mascara, and sparkly body glitter.

"Perfect," Blake says, once we're ready and looking at each other in the mirror. "Now for the surprise."

She runs over to her nightstand and pulls out a small black box, then opens it. A delicate silver charm bracelet slides out into her hand. A silver heart carved with the letter *A* is hanging off one of the small links. Then Blake pulls out another bracelet, this one identical, only with a small silver *B* on it.

"I wanted us to have something together," she says. "You know, like sisters do."

"I love it!" I exclaim. "But I feel so bad. It's your birthday, and I still haven't gotten you anything." I haven't found the perfect present for Blake yet. I want it to be special, since it's her first birthday after moving in with us. And a late present is better than a super-lame, right-on-your-birthday present, right?

"That's okay," she says. "I know whatever you get me will be amazing." She puts the charm bracelet on me, and I fasten hers to her wrist. Then we put them together and snap pics on our phones.

"Thanks, Blake," I say. "I really do love it."

"You're welcome," she says.

And then the doorbell rings.

"The guests are arriving," Blake says, her eyes shining with excitement. "Let's go."

Having a party is kind of weird, because you never really know what's going to happen. Like, you totally have to expect the unexpected. We've only been having this party for fifteen minutes, and already a bunch of craziness has taken place, including:

1. Gus eating my fruit sculpture. He just jumped right up on the counter and ate the whole thing. Now he's upstairs with my mom and Will, because they're afraid he might get sick or something. He doesn't seem sick, though. I can hear him whining because he wants to get back down and be where the action is. I wasn't even that upset about it. That he ate the whole sculpture, I mean. It didn't exactly turn out the way I was hoping. And besides, I realized pretty quickly that people were going to be way more interested in the chips and dip.

2. Jess showed up wearing a miniskirt, with no glasses and, like, five pounds of makeup on her face. I think she might have changed at Rina's

house, because no way her parents would ever let her out of the house like that.

3. Pretty much everyone we invited came. Except for Sam. He's not here yet, which is weird, because I know for a fact that he's spending the weekend at his grandma's house. I know this because I kind of sort of saw his mom's car sitting there this morning while I was taking Gus for a walk. It wasn't *my* fault that Gus was loitering all around their mailbox. I can't control him, he's crazy. And while Gus was doing that, I might have kind of sort of seen Sam in there through the window. Which wasn't even really spying, because like I said, Gus was sitting outside and not even trying to disguise the fact that he wouldn't come when I called him.

Anyway, the party's barely started, and there have already been a few scandals, and I guess they're going to keep on coming, because when the doorbell rings again, it's not Sam. It's Sophie Burns.

I can hear her voice upstairs as my mom answers the front door. We don't have the music on yet, because there's some kind of weird thing going on with the iPod, and Blake's kind of freaking out about it. Also, my mom totally insisted on opening the door for everyone. She said it's so we won't have to keep running up and down the stairs from the family room to the front door, but I think it's really because she wants to check out who's coming to this party.

"Oh, Sophie," I hear her say. "I didn't know you were coming tonight."

"Of course," Sophie says. "And I brought a fruit sculpture."

A fruit sculpture! Ohmigod. But how did she . . . Someone must have told her that I was making one! That little brat! I can't believe it! Blake is going to flip out. Like, really flip out.

I rush over to Blake. She tosses her hair over her shoulder and smiles at Jeremy Hairston, who's helping her with the iPod. "I don't understand how that could have happened," she's saying. "I always update my software. It's, like, my number one priority."

I've never heard anything about Blake updating her software, so I'm thinking she's just saying this because Jeremy is super into computers. Of course, I don't know everything about her, so she could totally be into updating constantly, but I kind of doubt it. Plus, it doesn't matter since we have way bigger problems right now.

"Blake," I say sweetly. "Can I talk to you for a second?"

"In a minute," she says, and then sets her iPod back into the dock. Music comes blaring out of the speakers, and she smiles.

"There," Jeremy says. "All set."

"Yup," she says. "All set." She's looking up at him from under lowered lashes.

Does Blake like Jeremy now? What happened to her liking Sam? Whatever, no time to think about that now.

"Blake!" I yell to be heard over the music, which she has at way too high of a volume. How are people supposed to talk? "Um, can you come here for a second?"

"What?" she asks, seemingly annoyed. But she follows me over to the corner of the room.

"Okay, I'm going to tell you something now," I say. "And I really don't want you to freak out."

"Is Sam here?" she asks, looking toward the door.

"No," I say. Why is she looking so hopeful? She was just practically throwing herself at Jeremy. "We have a problem. A big one."

"What's the problem?" She's already glancing over her shoulder, ready to get back to the party.

"Well—"

But the door to the family room opens before I can say anything, and Sophie comes walking into the room. Well, prancing is more like it. Seriously, the girl looks like she thinks she's on a catwalk or something.

My mom comes walking in behind her, holding the craziest fruit sculpture I've ever seen. It looks like a bouquet of flowers, with little pineapple petals and grapes for the middle. Geez. Mine looked nothing like *that*. It was just a scooped-out watermelon that was supposed to look like a basket but didn't, filled with melon balls.

Next to me, Blake gasps. "But she wasn't invited!" she says, a little louder than she should. A couple of girls from my French class turn around to look, and I try to quickly give them a reassuring smile, but they smirk at each other, like they know there's going to be some good drama on the way.

"Look," I say to Blake, lowering my voice so that the drama-mongers don't hear. "Yes, she's crashing. But she wants us to freak out. So what you have to do is pretend you invited her."

"I'm not pretending I invited her!" Blake exclaims. "I'm going to march over there and kick her out of this party immediately!"

"You can't do that," I say. "If you do, she's going to love it." Blake bites her lip, and I can see her weighing the options. On one hand, she can't stand that Sophie is here, and she really wants to give her a piece of her mind. On the other hand, if she makes a big fuss, Sophie will feel like she's won. I mean, Sophie so totally wants Blake to freak out on her. In the end, I decide for her. No way that Sophie Burns is ruining my first boy/girl party.

"Hello, Sophie!" I trill from the corner, waving my fingers at her. "How wonderful that you could come!" I take the fruit sculpture from my mom. "And what's this, a fruit sculpture? It looks just like a bouquet of flowers. How clever!"

A look of confusion passes over Sophie's face, but she recovers quickly. The rest of the guests, sensing nothing is going to happen, turn back to talking to each other, disappointed. It's like Sophie's just another person who's been invited to the party. In fact, people probably figure that we actually did invite her. It's not that weird. Sophie is on again, off again with so many people, everyone probably just figures that she's friends with me and Blake again.

"Yes, of course," Sophie says. "Even though I've been super busy getting things ready for my own party, I knew I had to stop by." She makes it sound like it was a last-minute decision, and that she's just passing through because of her busy schedule, but she's probably been planning this forever.

My mom sets the fruit sculpture down on the coffee

table and then raises her eyebrows at me, as if to say, *Are you okay?*

In response, I grab a piece of some exotic-looking fruit (is that a mango?) off the top of the bouquet and pop it into my mouth. "Thanks for carrying this, Mom," I say.

"You're welcome," she says, not quite knowing what to make of the whole scene. In the end, she refills the chip bowls and then walks back upstairs, glancing over her shoulder as she goes.

"So!" Blake says. "I'm so glad you could make it. For a second people thought you weren't going to show, because they thought we had some kind of weird party war going on. But there's totes enough parties for both of us!"

I take another grape out of the fruit sculpture and chomp on it. Sophie totally didn't even make this fruit sculpture. I saw the exact same one online while I was Googling recipes. It's from this company called Edible Arrangements or something. But whatevs. It's worth it to see Sophie trying to recover as Blake leads her over to the other side of the room and asks her what song she'd like to hear.

Someone taps me on the shoulder, and I'm so jumpy that I scream. "Ahhh!"

"Sorry," Rina says, giving me a strange look. "What's up with you?"

"Nothing," I say, smoothing my dress. "You just scared me, that's all."

"You need to calm down," Rina says. She hands me a cup of ginger ale, and I take a sip. "So let's go see your bridesmaid dress!" she exclaims, and I almost choke on my soda.

"Um, what?" I ask around the lump in my throat.

"Your dress!" she says. "The one you got for the wedding."

"Oh, right," I say, waving my hand like I've totally forgotten about it, even though I was kind of sort of boasting about it to Rina and Jess BTDD (Before The Dress Disaster). The fact that it's ruined now totally serves me right for being so braggy.

"Well, um, it's in my room, and my mom said no one's allowed upstairs." I shrug, like it's out of my hands. "Sorry."

"Come on," Rina says. "Your mom won't mind if I go up there. We can sneak away, just us. Jess is busy." I look over to the corner, where Jess is talking to Ben Crosby. She's giggling at something he's saying, then leans in and touches his arm. Wow. Who knew Jess was such a vixen?

"I can't," I say. I take another slow sip of my drink. "Sorry."

Rina's eyes narrow suspiciously. "What's going on?" she asks.

"What? What do you mean?"

"I mean, why are you acting so weird about your dress?"

"I'm not!" I say. "I'm not acting weird, I just—oh, look, there's Blake!" Blake's wandering by, a very strained look on her face. "Blake, what's wrong?" I grab her arm and pull her over to us.

"I'm going to kill Sophie," Blake says. She's smiling, but her teeth are gritted and she's talking through tight lips.

"Blake, why is Avery acting so weird about showing me her bridesmaid dress?" Rina asks, apparently not caring about the Sophie drama.

"Probably because I ripped mine and she spilled paint all over hers."

"Blake!" I shriek. "I thought we said we weren't going to tell anyone!"

"Rina won't tell anyone," Blake says. She looks toward the corner forlornly, where Sophie is now talking to Jeremy Hairston. "Besides, I have bigger problems." She grabs a strawberry, and then starts walking back toward the iPod.

"Why didn't you tell me?!" Rina asks. "You know I'm a master seamstress."

"You are?"

"Yes," she says, rolling her eyes. "My grandma taught me everything she knew. She owned her own sewing shop for, like, thirty years. Now, where's the dress?"

Fifteen minutes later I'm in my room, standing in front of my full-length mirror, twirling around in my dress. Rina insisted I put it on.

"Oh, Avery," she says, clapping her hands. "It's so gorgeous."

"I know," I breathe. Yes, there's paint on the bottom, but if you look at me without your eyes getting drawn to the big green splotch, it really is beautiful. Not to mention the dresses are a lot easier to appreciate now that Rina said she can fix them. She can sew Blake's dress, and apparently she has some super stain-remover recipe her grandma perfected that's safe for all fabrics and is going to get the paint out of mine. It makes me kind of sad, honestly. This whole time Rina was willing to help me, and I never even thought about asking her. Probably because I always feel like her and Jess are BFFs, and I'm the odd one out. But just because they're BFFs doesn't mean we're not really good friends. I need to give them more of a chance.

Anyway, we plan to sneak the dresses out of here in some gym bags, just in case my mom sees her leaving.

That way we can just tell her I'm letting Rina borrow some of my clothes. Which technically isn't even a lie.

"You're *sooo* lucky to get to wear a dress like that," she says. "You look just like a princess."

"You do," comes a voice from the doorway. I turn around to see Sam standing there, IN MY ROOM, his eyes wide as he looks at me in the dress.

"Sam!" I yell. "What are you doing up here? The party's in the family room!" I feel my cheeks getting hot, hot, hot. It's one thing for Rina to see me in my dress; it's another for an actual boy to see me in it. I mean, I know there are going to be boys at the wedding, but an actual boy who's my age, who I like, is completely different. Not to mention if he'd come in, like, two seconds earlier he would have seen me twirling all around, pretending I was on *America's Next Top Model* or something. Oh, God. Did he see that? How long has he been standing there?!

"I was looking for you," he says. "Jess told me she saw you and Rina come up here."

"Well, you have to go," I say, grabbing him by the shoulders and steering him toward the door. "You can't look at me in the dress." Then I remember about the paint stains on the bottom. "And besides, this dress is wrecked with paint. But Rina's going to fix it, so it won't be so messed up anymore, and Gus did it, but I'm not mad at him anymore." Wow. Way to babble.

"So what's what he did that was so bad," Sam says, laughing and shaking his head. "Well, you look really beautiful, Avery," he says. "I'll, um, see you downstairs."

"Ohmigod," Rina says once he's gone. She has a totally scandalized look on her face.

"He flirts with everyone," I say, rolling my eyes. "It doesn't mean anything."

"True," Rina says. Which kind of hurts my feelings. Because he must have meant it a little bit, right?

eleven

I CHANGE BACK INTO MY PARTY DRESS
and head back down to the family room, and once I'm
there, Sam comes up to me immediately. I'm hoping he
won't say anything about just having seen me in the bridesmaid dress (hello, embarrassing!) and/or the fact that I
was pretending to parade around like I was on a catwalk.

But all he says is, "So, what's Sophie Burns doing here?"

"Um, she just showed up," I say. "And so we're pretending she was invited."

"Genius," he says. "Who ordered the fruit sculpture?"

He breaks off a piece of watermelon and eats it.
"Sophie," I say. "And she's pretending that she made it."

"Really? That's bold." He reaches into the sculpture
and pulls out one of the fruit flowers. He holds it out to
me and grins. "Wanna dance?"

I glance over to the other side of the room, where Blake is still messing around with the iPod. I grab Sam's hand and pull him around the corner, up the stairs, and into the front hallway. "You have to stop," I say.

"Stop what?"

"This." I gesture at the flower.

"You don't like fruit?" He takes a bite.

"No, I do—I mean, no—" I take a deep breath. "I like fruit, yes. But I don't like you giving it to me."

"You don't like me back," he says, his face falling. "I get it. I'm sorry, I just thought—"

"No, it's not that."

"You do like me back?"

"No," I say. "I mean, yes. I mean, I don't know." This is super confusing. My whole head is like spinning around and around and around. It feels like I just got off a roller coaster or something. Not that I've ever really been on a roller coaster. Just those kiddie ones they have at Canobie Lake Park. But I'd imagine this is kind of what it feels like when you get off.

Sam moves a step closer to me. I think about taking a step back, but to tell you the truth, I kind of like how close he is to me. Which definitely isn't good. I can't just be going around liking him being this close. I can see how green his eyes are, and smell the fabric softener on his shirt, and I have to close my eyes because I can't take it.

"Look," I say. "It's complicated, and I can't really get into it now, but you should really—"

But before I can finish my thought, Sam brushes his lips against mine. They're soft and perfect and it's my first kiss and ohmigod, ohmigod, ohmigod, I just had my first kiss. I look at him in shock. He smiles at me shyly, and I smile back. And then he kisses me again.

A really warm feeling starts in my head and moves down to my stomach and all through my toes. And then I glance over Sam's shoulder. And there's Sophie Burns, standing in my kitchen. She has a soda in one hand, a fruit flower in the other, and a big grin on her face.

The only thing worse than having your first kiss and having no one to share it with because your soon-to-be stepsister likes the person you had your first kiss with? Having one of your enemies see your first kiss with her own eyes.

Not that Sophie's really my *enemy*, per se. I mean, I never really did anything to make her mad, as far as I know. She just decided one day that I wasn't worthy of her friendship. And I never really did anything to retaliate, so it's not like we're at war or anything. And since she's frozen Blake out now too, there's no real reason for Sophie to even tell Blake about the kiss.

In fact, Sophie's probably forgotten all about it. That's how girls like that are. They just forget about anything that doesn't have to do with them. Like the time I sprained my ankle getting out of Sophie's tree house in sixth grade, and then when I brought it up again at the end of the year, she'd totally forgotten that it had happened.

So she probably doesn't even remember the fact that she saw me kissing Sam. Or Sam kissing me. Ohmigod. Sam kissed me! I've been kissed! It's kind of crazy when you think about it. I wonder if he liked it as much as I did. I mean, I never knew kissing was so fun. I kind of want to do it again. (Not that I will.)

Anyway, after Sophie saw Sam kiss me, she turned around and walked back to the party and didn't say a word about it for the rest of the night. At first I thought that meant she was just saving it up to torture me with later, as she's been known to do with certain things. So all weekend, every time my or Blake's cell phone rang, I'd jump, just waiting for it to be Sophie, threatening to tell everyone what she saw.

But as the whole weekend went on and nothing happened, I kind of started to think that maybe she didn't care. And now it's already Monday morning at school, and I'm starting to think that she *really* didn't care, because she hasn't said a word to me. Which I'm totally thankful for, even though Sam hasn't really said a word to me either. Me and Sam are kind of, um, fighting. After we kissed and I saw Sophie staring at us, he turned around to see what I was looking at.

"Well, I guess we're going to be the talk of the school on Monday," he said. He grinned again, which I guess meant it was no big deal to him, since he's kind of used to being the talk of the school. But to me it was a big deal, since:

1. I'm so not used to being the talk of the school.
2. I don't want to ever be the talk of the school.
3. If Blake finds out Sam and I kissed, she will freak out and never talk to me again. Seriously, it could be that bad. I know it sounds dramatic, but I saw on this episode of *Oprah* once where these blended families were, like, torn apart by the two stepsisters fighting all the time. The parents were even thinking about getting a divorce over the whole thing. What if my mom and Will start thinking like that? That if we can't get along, they just don't want to deal

with us? What if they decide to call off the wedding? I can't be responsible for that! It would
be horrible.

And I told Sam all that, but he thought I was being
dramatic, and he was all, "Why don't you just tell Blake
that we like each other?" And then I said I couldn't,
because Blake was going to be my sister, and I could
never live with myself if our drama messed up my mom's
wedding next weekend. Anyway, so Sam and I got in
kind of a fight, and then he stalked back to the party and
didn't talk to me for the rest of the night. Which I guess
means that we're not talking.

So anyway, on Monday, during gym, I'm a little on
edge. Sophie's in my class, and she's acting the same
as always, her blond ponytail bouncing jauntily on her
head. Sophie always puts her long blond hair in a ponytail for gym class. A really tight one that she holds in
place with a sparkly rainbow hair tie. On anyone else it
would look kind of ridiculous, but on her, it looks really
good. It shows off her highlights, which she says are
natural, but there's no way they are.

"Line up in your groups!" Coach is yelling. Today he's
making us do gymnastics, which is so not fun when
you're like me and have no sense of balance at all. "Stay

in your group and use each apparatus for free play!"
"Free play" is what Coach calls it when he wants to be left alone so he can work on coming up with strategies for the boys' wrestling team. He stands in the corner and sketches out moves in his notebook, and we practice on the balance beam, uneven bars, and floor exercise.

I line up with my group in front of the balance beam. Sophie's in my group, and I can hear her behind me, talking loudly to a couple of girls she's friendly with, Emma Walker and Kenzie Prazo. "I know, my dad was like, we should totally get a fire eater, and I was like, Dad, no, that's wayyyy too much."

"What is she talking about?" Rina asks me. Rina's not in my group, so technically she's supposed to be on the uneven bars, but since Coach pays no attention to where anyone is, it doesn't really even matter that much.

"Her party," I say. "All she wants to do is talk about her party, party, party, party. It's so stupid. The party's not even for her, she's supposedly throwing it for Kaci."

"Is she really having a fire eater?"

"No," I say as the line inches forward. "Didn't you hear the part about how her dad wanted her to but she said no? She's trying to make out like she's the one who's turning down all these fabulous things, like she doesn't want to go over the top. But meanwhile she really just wants people to be like, 'Ohmigod, you were going to have a fire eater, you and your dad are so cool!'"

Rina nods her head. "She really is ridiculous."

"Completely." The line inches forward toward the balance beam, and I fidget with my hands. "So, um, are you sure the dresses are all set?"

"Yes," Rina says, sighing. "For the millionth time. I stayed up, like, all night last night finishing them. And they look as good as new."

"As good as new? You're sure?"

"*Yes.*"

It's not that I don't trust Rina. It's just that it's really, really, important the dresses are fixed. It's a little scary that she's been working on them, like, out of my sight, where she could have been doing anything to them. What if she made them worse without thinking she made them worse? Like when my mom tried to fix her at-home hair dye with another hair dye that turned her forehead purple.

"And your mom's going to drop them off after school, right?" I ask. I couldn't risk Rina bringing the dresses to school (what if they got lost and/or something happened to them?), and she couldn't drop them off at my house in case my mom was around, so she's going to drop them off at Angeline's, and then Blake and I are going to pick them up. Blake called Angeline last night and arranged the whole thing, swearing her to secrecy.

"*Yes*," Rina says. "Again, for the millionth time, yes, yes, yes."

"Avery!" Sophie yells. "Can you come up here and show me the right way to mount?"

Uh-oh. I look at Rina, and she looks back at me and shrugs. She has no idea about what happened with Sam and me, and what Sophie saw. I take a deep breath and go over to the balance beam. It's so totally obvious what's going on, since I'm not good at any kind of gymnastics, much less the balance beam, which takes all kinds of strength and agility and, you know, balance.

"So I always forget," she says. "What kind of mount do we do?"

Something tells me "Um, I don't know" is not going to fly, so I make something up.

"You just hoist yourself up like this." She nods, then grabs the beam and pulls herself up beautifully, not even really listening to what I told her to do. Which makes sense, since what I told her was definitely not right.

"Get up here next to me," she commands.

I sigh and then do it. "So, listen," she says, leaning in close to me so that no one else can hear. "I think you need to tell Ms. Tosh that you messed with the matches."

"That I what?" A sick feeling starts in my stomach. A horrible, disgusting, sick feeling that begins to move through my whole body, paralyzing me.

She smiles. "My dad's on the school board, and he told me how someone messed with the results. They're going to be doing this whole investigation. Obviously you're the one who did it. You were in charge of the whole project, and you wanted revenge on me for ditching you. Why else would I have been hooked up with *Taylor Meachum*?" She wrinkles her nose, like she can't even believe how ridiculous it is.

I swallow the sick feeling rising in my throat, and think of what I'd say to her if I were innocent. "I don't know why you'd end up with Taylor Meachum," I say. "Maybe because you guys are both awful?"

I figure being snotty will show her I'm not afraid and that I have nothing to hide. But it doesn't really work that way. Because instead of backing off, Sophie raises one side of her mouth back up into this really evil smile and says, "I'll give you a week to tell Ms. Tosh, or I'm going to tell Blake that you kissed Sam."

twelve

I DIDN'T EVEN KNOW IT WAS POSSIBLE, but somehow, the day keeps getting worse and worse. During eighth period, I get called down to Ms. Tosh's room. So does Sam. I've been avoiding him all day, and now not only am I going to have to see him, I'm going to have to see him while maybe possibly getting kicked off student council. Does Ms. Tosh know what I did? Should I tell her? Am I going to be found out anyway? If it means keeping my kiss with Sam a secret from Blake, then I'll definitely confess. The only problem is that I don't trust Sophie as far as I can throw her. Which means that even if I *do* tell Ms. Tosh that I was the one who used the manual override to enter some of the matches, Sophie might tell Blake anyway. In fact, she probably will.

Which means if I can somehow convince Ms. Tosh it wasn't me, and then tell Blake what happened, it might be okay. I don't want to lie to Blake, and there's definitely a better chance of her not being mad if she hears about the kiss from me. And if I *do* tell Blake, maybe, just maybe, Sophie will keep her mouth shut about the matches. She won't have anything on me anymore, and she won't be able to prove I was the one who did it anyway.

"So," Ms. Tosh says when we're sitting down in her classroom, "the IT department was able to figure out who went into the computer and switched the names." She looks over her glasses at us, her eyes serious. "And it seems like it was one of you."

"*What?*" Sam asks, leaning forward. Good actor, that Sam. If I didn't know any better, I'd think he really did believe it wasn't me.

"Yeah, what?" I ask, trying to arrange my features into a mask of confusion.

"The manual override happened while you two were in the computer lab, putting together the matches." She slides another paper across the desk, like she did last time, only this time, it has the time and date of the manual override, and the fact that it came from the computer I was using that day. "I'm assuming that neither one of you let someone else into the room while you were doing the matches. Is this true?"

"Yes," I say.

"Yes," Sam says.

"So that means either one or both of you did this," she says. "And since your names are both on the list of students on whom the manual override was used, it would make sense."

She looks back and forth between the two of us, her eyes turning from serious to steely. Suddenly I feel like I'm going to cry. I'm not used to getting in trouble at school. And when I say I'm not used to it, I mean that it's never happened. Ever before in my life.

"I'll give you both some time to let me know who's responsible for this while I talk to Mr. Standish, and then I'll tell you how we're going to proceed."

She nods at both of us, and we stand up and walk out of the room. I can't believe she's getting the principal involved!

We don't say anything as we walk down the hall, until we get to Sam's locker, and then he whirls around. "So," he says. "Was it worth it?"

"Was it worth it?" I repeat, confused. What is he talking about?

"Yeah," he says. "Acting like you want nothing to do

with me after I kissed you, just so you can keep up some lie that you have going with Blake."

"It's not a lie," I say.

"It *is* a lie," he says. "We kissed. And you haven't told her. That's a lie." I know he's right. And I really don't want to hear it. So I just turn around and keep walking.

"I don't get you," he says, following me. This is starting to become a pattern with us, me saying something he doesn't like and him following me. "I mean, I think you like me. And Blake . . . I mean, I get it, kind of . . . but . . . I don't know." He looks at me, and I turn my eyes to meet him. "I like you," he says softly, so softly it makes my heart ache. "I like you a lot. But if you don't want to be honest with me or with Blake, if you want to keep pretending, then I don't know how we can even be friends."

I want to tell him that I do want to be honest with him, that I like him a lot too, that I can't stop thinking about how he kissed me, that I want to kiss him again, that my stomach gets all sparkly and bubbly every time he's around me, like there's fireworks going off in there, the really good, Fourth of July kind.

But if I have to tell Blake I kissed Sam, it's going to be a million times worse if I have to also tell her that I still like him. The only chance I have of her forgiving me is to pretend that nothing's going on with us. So instead, I just say, "No, I told you . . . I don't . . . Look, it doesn't really matter what I feel. Blake likes you, and that's the end of it."

"Are you sure?"

"Yes," I say. "I'm sure. Kissing you was a mistake."

I turn around and walk away, and this time, he doesn't follow me.

"So do you really think they're going to look okay?" I ask nervously. It's after school, and me and Blake are standing on Angeline's porch, about to pick up the dresses that Rina dropped off a little while ago.

"I dunno," Blake says, shrugging. She reaches out and rings the doorbell. "I guess we'll find out." Wow. Way to be comforting.

"Girls!" Angeline says, pulling open the door. "Come in, come in!" She looks around furtively, like she's afraid someone might have tailed us here. I look behind her too, really hoping I don't see Sam. Even though I made sure to double-check that he was staying after for lacrosse practice, I'm still a little nervous. No way do I want to run into him after what happened today.

We traipse through Angeline's living room and into the kitchen. The whole kitchen smells like something yummy, maybe lasagna or meatballs. There's a pot bubbling away on the stove, and Angeline leads us over to the table where our dresses are draped over a chair. She holds them up, and Blake and I lean in.

And then I let out a huge sigh of relief. There's no sign of paint or rips or anything! I'm so excited that I start jumping up and down. "They're fixed, they're fixed, they're fixed!" I grab Blake's hands and twirl her around the kitchen.

"Stop," she says, giggling. "You're making me all dizzy."

"They look lovely," Angeline says, folding them carefully and packing them in the gym bags we brought. "Just make sure to steam them with your mom's steamer when you get home." The gym bag was part of our cover story. We figured if Will or my mom asked us where we were going, we could just tell them that we were going out for a run on the track at the park. We can also just bring the dresses home in the bags without having to worry about covering them up. Who knew gym bags would always be coming in so handy? Of course, if my mom or Will *had* seen us, they probably would have asked why we weren't bringing the dogs with us if we were going out running. Which is why we had to. Bring the dogs with us, I mean.

They're sniffing around at my feet. Actually, that's not completely true. Gus is sniffing the air. His nose is pointing straight up, taking in the scents of the yummy Italian food.

"You brought the dogs," Angeline says. "How wonderful." But it doesn't really sound like she thinks it's too wonderful.

"They love meatballs," Blake offers helpfully.

"Yes, well, those meatballs won't be done for another couple of hours," Angeline says. Which is probably a lie, since I'm pretty sure meatballs don't take that long to cook. But maybe the kind she makes does. Something tells me she's not just pulling them out of a bag in the freezer and dropping them into a pot like we do at our house.

Angeline looks at the dresses, then looks down at Gus warily. "Maybe those dogs would like to go in the backyard," she says.

"Gus," I ask, "do you want to go in the backyard?" Which is ridiculous, since of course dogs don't speak English. And even if they were somehow able to figure it out, Gus still probably wouldn't know what I'm talking about. He's not that smart. But surprisingly, he actually starts to wag his tail. So I lead him and Princess into the backyard, where Gus starts running around and chasing after leaves, and Princess starts sniffing around at the grass, like she wants to make sure that she knows what she's getting herself into before committing to actually walking around the yard. Dogs are so weird.

"So, girls," Angeline says once we're back in the kitchen. "You must taste this."

She pulls out two bowls and ladles some sauce into them, then cuts big chunks of Italian bread off a loaf that's sitting on the counter. "Dip," she instructs.

We do, and the hot, spicy sauce explodes in my mouth. Ohmigod. Delicious. "This is sooo good," I say.

"Amazing," Blake says. Then she looks at Angeline seriously. "You know you can't tell anyone about the dresses, right? That this is to be a complete and total secret, especially from Avery's mom?"

"I know and I promise," Angeline says, making a cross over her heart.

The front door slams open, and we hear Sam's voice come floating through the kitchen. "Gram!" he yells. "I'm here!" He walks into the room, but stops short when he sees me and Blake sitting there, eating sauce. "Oh," he says. "Sorry, I didn't know you had company. Practice was canceled, so I figured I'd stop by before Mom got home."

"Rina dropped our dresses off here so my mom

wouldn't find out, and now we're trying your grandma's sauce," I say, pointing at our bowls.

"That's great." He smiles, but it doesn't reach his eyes. It's the kind of smile you give when you're just tolerating someone. It's the kind of smile I gave to Sophie Burns when she showed up at my house to hang out with Blake. The kind of smile you give someone when they're really making you mad and they're the last person in the world you want to see. And in that second, I think about kissing him, about how badly I want to do it again, and how mad he is at me, and suddenly I'm not really that hungry anymore.

"We should go," I say to Blake.

"But we just got here," she says, smiling all flirty at Sam. "And I want more of this delicious sauce."

Angeline beams, then picks up Blake's bowl and ladles another big scoop into it.

"Sit," she tells Sam. "You need to eat." She looks at the three of us. "You three are all too skinny. Kids these days are all too skinny." She clucks in disapproval and starts making up a bowl for Sam.

"So," Blake says. She twirls a lock of hair around her finger and leans in closer to Sam, probably so he can smell her perfume. "How's everything with you?"

"Good," Sam says. "Same old, same old." He glances

at me out of the corner of his eye. "Just busy with some student council stuff." My heart starts to race a little. Why did he have to bring *that* up? Is he trying to imply that he's going to tell on me? "That's why I was late getting home, even though my practice was canceled," he says. "I had to take the late bus since I stayed after to talk to Ms. Tosh about something."

I take a deep breath and push my bowl away. "I should go," I say. "I have a lot of homework."

"I'll go with you," Blake says, standing up reluctantly.

"No," I say. "It's okay . . . you should stay."

"Are you sure?"

"Yeah, I'm just going to grab the dogs and go home."

And that's exactly what I do.

Two hours. That's how long Blake stays over at Angeline's house with Sam. Two. Whole. Freaking. Hours. Who knows what they're doing in that time? Homework? Talking? Eating? Making out? All of the above?

I allow myself a little imagined conversation between the two of them, just to drive myself completely crazy.

It goes like this:

> Sam: So listen, I heard your dad's wedding
> is coming up. Maybe I could be your date.

Blake: Oh, that would be so great! I
wonder if Avery would feel bad, though.
I don't think she has a date.

Sam: Okay, so, confession. I used to
like her, but not anymore. She's kind of
a loser now, since she tried to rig the
matchmaking project.

Blake: She tried to rig it?!

Sam: Yeah, but I told on her, so now she's
probably going to get kicked off student
council.

Blake: Well, it's probably good that
someone takes her down a peg.

Sam: For sure. (They kiss and smile, happy
that they're together now, and deciding
not to pay any attention to me and my
fragile self-esteem.)

I try to distract myself, but a bunch of different ver-
sions of this scenario insist on running through my

mind, including one where Angeline decides to tell my mom all about the ruined dresses. (She doesn't tell her that Blake had anything to do with it, since now that Blake and Sam are probably going to be married, Blake will be family someday, and Angeline can't turn her back on family—in this version, she even invites Blake over to teach her how to make their secret family recipe spaghetti sauce.)

I call Rina, but she doesn't answer, and it's not like I could tell her what was going on anyway. I try to do my homework, but all my math problems are swimming together, and I can't even do simple addition without getting distracted. I try to Google some interesting interior design ideas, but all the colors are bleeding into one, and I can't concentrate.

When the front door finally opens and Gus and Princess start barking, I'm this close to driving myself completely and utterly crazy.

"Hey," Blake says, rushing into the room. Her cheeks are flushed with happiness, and a few stray strands of hair are falling out of her ponytail. She looks great.

"Hi," I say. "How was it?"

"Hanging out with Sam?" she says. "It was amazing. We did our homework, and then Angeline gave us cheesecake for dessert." She pats her stomach. "I'm going to end up gaining, like, ten pounds if I keep hanging out over there." Keep hanging out over there? As in more than once? As in a lot? Who said anything about that?

"That's good," I say. I pretend I'm totally consumed with some purple patterned curtains online. "Do you think you'll be over there a lot now?"

"Well, I don't know," she says. "It depends on how things go between us." She stops. "Do you think it would be crazy to ask him to be my date at the wedding?"

"Umm . . ." I stare at the pattern of the curtains on my screen, and feel hot tears swim to the front of my eyes. I blink them back as the screen starts to go a little bit blurry. "Well, I'm not really sure if we're allowed to have dates."

"Well, no one said we couldn't, did they?"

"No, but you know that they have to pay for each plate and everything, right?"

"Right," Blake says. She's over at the mirror in the middle of the room, and has picked up earrings from my dresser and is trying them on. My earrings! Putting them right in her ears like it's nothing. I know I wanted to share everything with her, but that was before I realized that she likes the same boy I like. The same boy who is supposed to like me too. "But it's not too late to add a couple more people," she says. "I asked Angeline, since she's the caterer."

"You asked Angeline?" I say, swiveling around on my computer chair. "Does she know you want to ask Sam?"

"Of course not," she says, taking the earrings out of her ears and moving on to my necklaces. She holds a turquoise drop necklace up to her neck, then puts it back down. What, like my necklaces aren't good enough for her or something? I mean, geez.

"What's wrong with that necklace?" I ask.

"What?" She's distracted, picking up the next one and fastening it around her neck. She ignores my question and says, "So anyway, I was thinking you could ask Kevin Hudson."

"Kevin Hudson?" I ask warily.

"Yeah, you like him, don't you?"

"Sort of," I say. Not really anymore. But maybe I should start liking him. Now that I've blown it with Sam, maybe I should go back to liking Kevin Hudson. I mean, I liked him before, when I thought Sam was ridiculous and conceited and crazy. And just because I started to like Sam, that doesn't mean that Kevin is any less worth liking. Does it? Plus, think about how great it would be to ask Kevin as my date before I told Blake that I kissed Sam. She probably wouldn't mind as much if it was obvious that I liked someone else, and if she and Sam were getting together.

"Then you should ask him," she says. She turns around, the turquoise necklace back on her neck. "Can I borrow this tomorrow? I want to look extra special when I ask Sam to the wedding."

"Shouldn't we make sure it's okay with my mom and your dad first? You know, to bring dates?"

She shrugs. "It's better this way. We can just ask the boys tomorrow and then bring it up to our parents at dinner."

"Sounds perfect!" Not.

"So can I borrow your necklace?"

"Sure." I mean, why not? She's already about to borrow my crush.

thirteen

REASONS I SHOULD ASK KEVIN HUDSON
to the wedding:

1. He is very cute, and always has smart things to say in social studies, like the time he brought up the fact that the majority of Muslims are very into peace, when we were having a debate on the construction of a mosque near Ground Zero.
2. He always used to give me the cookies from his lunch in fourth grade.
3. He's nice to everyone.

   Reasons I should not ask Kevin Hudson to the wedding:

1. I don't want to.
2. He's not Sam.

"There he is," Blake says the next day. We're filing into the auditorium for an assembly, and it's kind of pandemonium. We're supposed to be sitting with our homerooms, but it's hard to keep everyone together, so as long as you're in the general vicinity of where you're supposed to be, the teachers don't really care. Or if they do, they don't have the energy to yell at us about it.

"There's who?" I ask, even though I already know who she's talking about. All morning Blake has been texting me, asking me if I've asked Kevin to the wedding yet. When I say no, she keeps saying, "When are you going to do it?" Apparently she's just dying to ask Sam, but she hasn't seem him yet, so she hasn't.

"Kevin," she says. She pushes me toward him. "Go on, ask him to the wedding."

"Not here!" I say. Is she crazy? If I'm going to be forced into asking a guy I'm not even sure I like anymore to go with me to my mom's wedding (where I'm not even sure I'm allowed to bring a date), I'm certainly not going to do it here, in front of the whole school.

"Here is as good a place as any," she says. Then she stands on her tiptoes so she can see over everyone's head and screams, "Hellllo! Kevin! Over here!"

"What are you doing?" I say, grabbing the sleeve of her sweater and trying to pull her back down to normal height. She doesn't even know Kevin! To my knowledge, they've never even spoken! Of course, they *were* matched up for the matchmaking disaster, so maybe they've actually taken care of that by—

"Hey," Kevin says, fighting his way back through the crowd and stopping when he gets to us.

Blake cocks her head and gives me a look, like, *See? Would he have come back here if he wasn't at least a little bit interested?*

Probably he would. Like I said, he's nice to everyone, and not the type to totally ignore someone when they're calling his name. Although I'm not sure what he would do if he knew someone wanted to ask him to be their date to their mother's wedding. Maybe he might ignore them then. I mean, what thirteen-year-old boy wants to get all dressed up and go to a dumb wedding? God, my life is really turning into a disaster.

"Hi," Blake says, after an awkward pause in which I'm assuming I was supposed to say something. "What's going on?"

"Nothing," he says. "Same old stuff. What's going on with you guys?"

"Oh," Blake says, standing up on her tiptoes again and looking out over the crowd. "There's my friend, waving to me. I have to go see what she wants."

"What friend?" Kevin asks, looking out over the crowd. He doesn't even have to get on his tiptoes, because he's so tall he can see over everyone.

"Uh, my friend," Blake says, waving her fingers good-bye at us. "Gotta go!" She gives me a look like, *Ask him or else!* and then gets swallowed up by the crowd. O-kaay. Whatever. This isn't even a big deal, when I think about it, because I don't even like Kevin. I used to, that's true, but not anymore. Now I just like Sam.

Kevin's still looking around like he has no clue what's going on. "What friend?" he asks. "Now she's just up there sitting by herself."

"Yeah, well, she has bad eyesight," I say, before I realize how stupid it sounds.

"Bad eyesight?" He frowns, like he's confused, and I shrug and point to my ears, like I can't hear him. Hopefully he'll think that he couldn't hear me, either, and that he totally misunderstood the bad eyesight comment.

"So anyway," I say once we're sitting down in the auditorium, in a couple of seats on the aisle, and it's a little more quiet. "How have you been?"

"Good," he says. "How have you been?"

"Fine." I look around, trying to think of something to say to him. "I got a dog," I blurt.

"Oh? That's cool." He turns and looks up at the stage, waiting for the assembly to begin. Wow. Great conversationalist, this one. You know what? I don't have to ask him to the wedding. Who cares if Blake goes with Sam? Just because she has a date doesn't mean that *I* have to have a date. We don't have to do *everything* together. If I don't have a date, it doesn't mean I'm a loser or anything. And granted, she is going to be asking the guy I like, but that doesn't mean he's going to say yes! She hasn't even asked him yet.

I turn around and face forward, happy with my new decision, just in time to see Blake turn around in her chair and look at me. "Ask him!" she mouths. I shake my head. No more Ms. Nice Guy. I'm not going to give into the peer pressure. But then Sam comes walking down the aisle. He meets my eyes and then looks away. I see Blake waving him over, and then Sam goes and sits down next to her. Well, then.

"So," I say to Kevin. "My mom's getting married this weekend, and I was wondering if maybe you'd like to go with me. It wouldn't have to be a date or anything, it would just be nice to go with someone. Blake's going to ask Sam, and it would be cool if I had someone to hang out with too."

He looks at me, and a flicker of surprise flashes across his face, but then he nods and says, "Sure, I'd love to go with you. Just text me all the details." The lights start to dim, and everyone quiets down.

Well. That wasn't so bad.

Blake comes running up to me as soon as the assembly is over. She's done a little braid on the side of her hair and clipped it back with a barrette like she does sometimes, and it looks really trendy and cute. She bounces up and down excitedly.

"Did you ask him, did you ask him?"

"Yes," I say. "Now, shhh, I don't want him to hear you." I look around, but Kevin is nowhere to be seen. Still. The last thing I want is for someone to notice Blake and be like, *"Did she ask who?"*

"He said yes, right?"

"Yeah," I say. I shuffle toward the auditorium doors, and once we're back out into the hall, I turn around and look at her. "So did you ask Sam?"

"No," she says. "But I'm going to next period." She looks at me, her eyes all shiny. "It will be a really big test, you know? Because if he says yes, that means he likes me. And if he says no, that means I have to move on."

"Move on?"

"Yeah," she says. "Maybe to Tristan Wells or something." She shrugs. "Anyway, see ya!"

And then she's gone.

Reasons that really *was* so bad:

   1. Kevin isn't Sam.

Waiting for the next period to be over is excruciating. I just keep thinking about the fact that Blake is, right at that moment, asking Sam to my mom's wedding. The answer could mean everything. If he really likes me, he would say no, right? And if he does say no, will Blake really move on? And if so, will I finally tell her about the kiss? Why *haven't* I told her about the kiss? I already asked Kevin to the wedding, he already said yes, so shouldn't I just TELL HER ABOUT THE KISS?

When the bell rings, I realize I haven't heard a word the teacher said. I gather up my things and send Blake a quick text. DID U ASK HIM?! WHAT DID HE SAY??? But she doesn't respond. And she keeps not responding for the rest of the day.

By the time I get home from school and I'm sitting at

the kitchen table, my books open in front of me, I'm freaking out. I tried to talk to Blake on the bus, but I couldn't, because she sat in the back with this super-pretentious girl named Rachel Fitzsimmons, who I didn't even know she was friends with. But that's the thing about Blake—she's always talking to tons of different people, and making friends with them, and just generally being . . . well, social. It's kind of annoying, actually.

Anyway, not only did Blake sit in the back with Rachel, but then she GOT OFF THE BUS AT HER HOUSE. Which isn't even allowed, you know, unless you have a bus pass, but I guess Blake didn't care. And apparently neither did our bus driver.

Finally, at around four o'clock, Blake comes waltzing through the front door and into the kitchen. "Are you—," I start, but she holds up her finger. And that's when I notice she's on her cell phone. "I know!" she's saying. "I can't believe it either! No, I can't this weekend, I'm going to be at my dad's wedding. Okay, I have to go. Okay . . . Okay . . . Bye!"

"So," I say as soon as she hits the button to end the call. "What did he say?"

"Who?" She opens the refrigerator and takes out a container of dip and a small bag of baby carrots, and then sits down at the table.

"Sam!" Is this girl for real?

"Oh, Sam," she says, then takes a dainty bite of carrot. She chews and then swallows, obviously not caring that I'm dying over here. "Well, he said he's going to be there."

I feel like someone punched me in the stomach, and my breath all whooshes out of me in one big gulp. "So you're going with him?" Visions begin dancing in my head. Horrible visions. Visions of all four of us—me, Kevin, Sam, and Blake—sitting at the table at my mom's wedding. Sam is feeding Blake some kind of delicious food that Angeline made, and then he asks her to dance. I watch from my seat as they slow dance on the dance floor, and then he reaches over and pushes her hair out of her face and leans down to kiss her.

"Well, yeah, I'm going," she says. "Obvi. And he's going too, but he was going to be there anyway."

"What do you mean?"

"I mean he was going to be there anyway." She picks up the container of dip and stares at the label. "Can you believe there's high-fructose corn syrup in this? In dip! That's ridiculous."

"Totally," I say, because it is. High-fructose corn syrup is in everything these days. "But what do you mean Sam's going to be there anyway?"

"He's going to be working there," she says. "Catering

for his grandmother. I guess he, like, passes out hors d'oeuvres or something. Isn't that so cute?"

"Yeah," I say honestly, "it is." I wonder what he has to wear. Probably black pants and white shirt. Maybe he even has to wear a tie! I bet he'd look supercute in a tie.

"Anyway, I guess he helps her out for events. He doesn't even want to get paid, but of course Angeline pays him anyway." She really knows a lot about their family. Annoying.

"So we're going to hang out there," she says. "So it's kind of like he's my date, even though he won't be able to sit at our table." She grins. Great. Now I'm going to be sitting at the head table with Kevin. And he's probably going to think it's a total lie that Blake was bringing a date, and that I wanted to ask him because I like him.

"That's great," I say brightly.

"Yeah," she says. She puts the top on the dip and puts it back in the fridge. "Also, you should probably ask your mom about all this." Right. My mom. Now that Blake technically isn't going to have a date, I'm going to have to ask my mom if I can bring one. When I didn't even want to in the first place.

"Um, well," I say slowly, "since you won't really be going with Sam, then maybe I should just tell Kevin to forget it."

"What do you mean I won't really be going with Sam?" Her eyes get a little stormy when she says it. Yikes.

"Not that you won't be *going* with him," I say quickly. "Just that he won't be sitting with us. At the table. So it would be weird if Kevin sat there. It would, you know, mess up the balance of the seating chart." The balance of the seating chart? Seriously, how do I come up with this stuff?

"I'm sure it will be fine," she says, looking at me strangely. "You still want to go with Kevin, don't you?"

"Of course," I say. Lie.

She nods like it's all settled. "Then you can ask your mom tonight."

fourteen

ASKING MY MOM IF I CAN BRING A DATE
to her wedding was beyond embarrassing. I really do
not want to even think about the details of the exchange
(maybe someday when I'm older I'll laugh about it, but I
doubt it). Anyway, it went something like this:

> Me (approaching my mom while she's
> sitting in the living room watching
> *Say Yes to the Dress*, this ridiculous
> show that follows all these totally
> spoiled brides as they pick out their
> wedding dresses): Mom, can I talk
> to you?
>
> Mom: Sure, honey. (still looking at the

TV) Can you believe she's going to
get that dress? The amount of lace
on it!

Me: Mom? It's kind of important.

Mom (switches off TV and sits at
attention): Honey, what is it?

(The door opens. Will comes walking in,
wearing shorts and a T-shirt, fresh from
his run outside.)

Will: What's up, guys?

Mom: Nothing. Avery was just getting
ready to talk to me about something
important.

Will (sits down on couch): Oh. (looks at
me) Is it serious?

Me: Um, well . . . (not wanting to hurt
his feelings) It's kind of more of a
girl thing.

Will (face gets red, probably because
he thinks it has to do with periods or
something): Oh, well, okay then. (jumps
up from couch) See you later! (runs to
kitchen)

Mom: Go ahead, sweetie.

Me: Well, the thing is . . . I was just
wondering if it would be okay if I asked
someone to the wedding.

Mom (frowning): Like Rina or Jess?
Honey, you know we had to give
Angeline the head count a couple of
days ago.

Me: Um, no, not Rina or Jess.

Mom: Who?

Me (face getting all hot): Uh, no one. I
mean, if you already put in the head
count and everything . . . (starting to back
up toward the door)

Mom: Wait a minute, Avery. Who did
you mean? (a small smile starts to play on
her lips)

Me: No one!

Mom: Sam?

Me: Sam! Sam who? Why would you think
that?

Mom: I don't know, it just seemed like
the two of you were really bonding over
the dogs.

Me: Um, no, it wasn't Sam. (realizing I
should tell her who it is, in case she lets
it slip to Will and/or Blake that she thinks
I've been "really bonding" with Sam) It's
this boy at school, Kevin Hudson.

Mom: Oh, right, Kevin Hudson. His mom
and I used to be room mothers together
in third grade. (looking at me with pride,
like she can't believe her little girl is old

enough to go on dates with a kid she
remembers from third grade) Of course
you can bring Kevin.

Me: But I thought you just said that you
already gave the head count.

Mom: I'm sure we can squeeze in one
more. (claps her hands together and
brings them to her chest) I cannot believe
that you're old enough to go on a date!
(tears come to her eyes) And on my
wedding day, too. Oh, honey, come here.
(holds her arms out for a hug)

Me (hugging her reluctantly): Mom, it's not
really that big of a deal.

Mom: Yes, it is. (sniffs and lets me go)

End Scene

I know. So totally embarrassing. I can't even look
at my mom for the rest of the night, because I'm afraid
she's going to get all sappy again. Not to mention that I

can't really look at Will either, because I just know my mom told him everything. Not that I have time to really dwell on the embarrassment that is now my life, since Friday morning at school, I get called down to Ms. Tosh's room. The only thing I can think of is that Sam told on me, and that's why she wants to talk, so I decide there's no way I'm going down to her classroom. I just need the weekend. I just need the weekend to get through the wedding, tell Blake about my kiss with Sam while somehow convincing her that I don't like him anymore, and then come up with some kind of really good and plausible story about how I wasn't the one who mixed up the matches.

I'm able to avoid Ms. Tosh all day, even though she has me paged down to the office and to her classroom two more times. At one point she's coming down the hall at the same time I am, and I have to duck into the library to avoid her. (I know! It's so covert and crazy!)

It's like I have a merry-go-round of problems in my head—just when I'm forgetting about the embarrassing stuff having to do with asking my mom about a wedding date because of the stuff with Ms. Tosh, I have to forget about the stuff with Ms. Tosh because of the fact that the wedding is tomorrow and I'm going with Kevin and I really want to be going with Sam.

And of course Blake isn't really helping matters.

"Angeline won't return my calls," she seethes that night. We're standing out in the backyard with the dogs, supposedly trying to teach them how to play fetch (yeah, right—Gus will run after the ball but will never give it back to you, and Princess is way too snotty to ever play a game like fetch).

"What is she supposed to call you about?" I ask. When did they get to be such good friends?

"She's done with the surprise dish for the wedding," Blake says. "And I was supposed to go over there tonight and try it, but she hasn't called me back."

"I didn't know she was making a surprise dish for the wedding," I say, frowning.

"Yeah," she says. "We decided the other day when you and I went to pick up the dresses." *They* decided? I didn't know she and Angeline were a *they*. Unless she means her, Angeline, and Sam decided. Is that the "we" she's talking about?

I bite my lip. "How many messages did you leave her?"

"Four messages and seven texts."

Wow. Stalker much? Blake's phone rings before I have a chance to tell her she might want to lay off with the calls and texts. She looks down at the caller ID and then breathes a sigh of relief. "It's Sam," she says. Sam?

Why is *Sam* calling her? She said she left *Angeline* all the messages. They really are a "we," those three! God, could my life get any worse? Like, for real. "Hello? Yes, hi! Ohmigod, seriously! That's amazing, I'll be right over." She slides her phone shut and jumps up and down. "I'm going over," she says.

"Great," I say, waiting for her to invite me. But she doesn't.

She just reaches into her purse and studies her reflection in her compact. "I cannot believe what a mess I look!"

"You don't look a mess," I say honestly.

"Thanks," she says. "Okay, be back in a few." And she is back in a few. But not in a few minutes. More like a few hours.

fifteen

THE MORNING OF THE WEDDING IS BRIGHT
and clear, with a deep blue sky and a bunch of fluffy
clouds that look like big cones of white cotton candy. I
walk sleepily downstairs at 8:00 a.m. to find Will making us all chocolate toffee French toast.

My mom comes in behind me and gives him a kiss on
the lips. "Hello," she says. "Good morning."

My mom and Will decided not to do the whole "not
seeing each other before the wedding" thing. She said
it took her this long to find him, so she doesn't understand why she should spend time away from him when
she doesn't have to. Also I think they're both kind of
nervous about the ceremony and want to be with each
other for support, which is pretty cute.

By the time my mom, Will, and I finish our French

toast, Blake is still asleep, and so I go upstairs and work on some homework while I wait for her to wake up.

I'm almost done with my science when Kevin texts me. ALL SET FOR THE BIG DAY? ☺

YUP!

LOOKING FORWARD TO SEEING YOU!

ME TOO

When Blake finally wakes up, we pack up all our stuff and head over to the Harbor Point to get ready. Blake and I have a huge suite all to ourselves, and we take bubble baths in the Jacuzzi tub, then sit in big, fluffy robes and eat fruit from a cheese plate while we get our hair and makeup done.

The hairstylist pulls our hair back and then slides different strands all through this special ponytail holder that makes a bun with a very intricate design. When she's finished, it looks very cool and very complicated. Then we get our makeup done, and even get to put on fake eyelashes and sparkly body jewels that go on our shoulders and look very subtle but very fancy.

When it's time to walk down the aisle, Blake squeezes my hand.

"I'm really glad we're going to be sisters," she says.

"Me too," I say, squeezing back. I feel a little guilty,

thinking about the secret I'm still keeping from her, but I push it out of my mind, telling myself to enjoy the moment. I'll tell her after the wedding. Right now the only thing that's important is that everything goes perfectly for my mom and Will.

I'm only a little bit nervous walking down the aisle, and the ceremony is beautiful. I don't usually get all sentimental—I mean, I even kind of hate romantic comedy movies—but I get really choked up watching my mom and Will get married. I mean, I'm just so thrilled for them! I know my mom wasn't completely, 100 percent happy for a really long time, and now that she has Will, I feel like she finally is.

When the reception starts, I take my seat at the head table next to Kevin.

"Hey," he says, pulling my chair out for me. "That was a really nice ceremony."

"Thanks," I say, not sure boys are supposed to notice things like that. Of course, he probably didn't even *really* notice, he just thought it was the polite thing to say. He probably would have said the same thing even if he thought the ceremony sucked.

"So are you excited about the student council ski trip?"

Not really, I think, *since I'm about to get kicked out of student council.* "Totally," I say. I take a sip of water from the glass that one of the waiters put down in front of me. "I really love skiing." This part, at least, is true. I've only been once, but I really did love it. Sliding down the mountain on the snow, riding the ski lift . . . It's all really fun. Especially warming up next to the fire with a huge mug of hot chocolate.

Someone starts to fill my water glass, even though I've only taken one sip. "That's okay," I turn to tell the waiter. "You don't have to—"

"Hi, Avery," Sam says, meeting my eyes. He's wearing the exact waiter's uniform I thought he'd be wearing—black pants, a crisp white shirt, and a black tie. He smiles, but it's the same smile he gave me in Angeline's kitchen that day, the one that doesn't reach his eyes.

"Oh, hi, Sam," I say. "Blake said you'd be working here." I look around for Blake and spot her over on the other side of the room, talking to some relatives of hers that I've never met. "She's right over there."

"Hi, Kevin," Sam says cheerfully. "Did you enjoy the ceremony?"

"I thought it was beautiful," Kevin says.

"Yeah, I'll bet you did," Sam says, and in a not-very-friendly way. I take another sip of my water. "Do you guys want some hors d'oeuvres?" Sam asks. "They're going to be coming out soon, and I can make sure you get first pick."

"Uh, no," I say, a nervous feeling in my stomach. "That's okay."

"Actually, I'd love to have first pick of the appetizers," Kevin says, smiling at Sam. "I'm pretty hungry. I had wrestling practice this morning."

"Oh, yeah, wrestling practice must really take a lot out of you," Sam says. But he says it kind of sarcastically.

"It really does," Kevin says agreeably, totally not picking up on the sarcasm. "If you ever decide you don't want to play lacrosse anymore, you should try out."

I see Sam's eyes flash with annoyance, and I understand why. I mean, Kevin is kind of implying that lacrosse is so easy that if Sam ever decides he's done with it, maybe he should join a real sport like wrestling. Not only that, but he's making it clear that he'll have to try out, because who knows if he's even good enough to make it. I'm sure Kevin didn't mean it that way, but I can tell Sam's taking it that way. Yikes.

"Yeah, so, I'm glad you're going to take care of the appetizers," I say a little too loudly, mostly because at this point I just want to get rid of him. He looks like he's about two seconds away from punching Kevin or something, and I so can't be responsible for that happening at my mom's wedding.

"No problem," Sam says. "Be right back." I wait until he's gone, then turn back to Kevin, and quickly steer the convo back to the ski trip. But ten minutes later, Sam's still not back with the appetizers, which really seems to bother Kevin.

"He never came back," he keeps saying. "And I'm *really* hungry. I would have *really* liked to have had those appetizers."

"It's okay," I tell him. I rummage around in my purse and hand him some mints. "Have one of these."

Who knew that Kevin was actually a little bit of a drama queen? I mean, not to be mean or anything, but it's just an appetizer. Like, let it go, you know?

Finally he does let it go, right before it's time for the speeches. We listen to speeches from my aunt, Will's dad, and my mom's best friend, Bonnie. And then, finally, it's time for dinner. The food is delicious, yummy and spicy and just perfect.

While we're finishing up, the music starts, and Blake is the first one out on the dance floor, grabbing Sam's hand and pulling him after her, even though he's supposed to be clearing the tables. I watch them, a sick feeling in my stomach and a lump in my throat. When a slow song starts, Blake pulls Sam close to her and leans her head on his shoulder.

"You want to dance?" Kevin asks, following my gaze. I guess he's thinking that I have this look on my face because I want to be out there, not because I specifically want to be out there with Sam.

I'm about to say no, because there's nothing I'd rather do less than be out there dancing while the boy I'm maybe kind of sort of in love with (okay, that's dramatic, but he *is* the biggest crush of my life so far) is out there dancing with my soon-to-be stepsister. Although now she's not even my soon-to-be stepsister. Now she's my real, honest-to-goodness stepsister. But then I start to get a little angry. I mean, I *should* be out there. It's my mom's wedding. I shouldn't let stupid Sam Humphrey ruin my fun! This might be one of the last times I'll even be able to have fun, since after this I'm going to be off student council, and Blake is going to hate me.

So I grab Kevin's hand and pull him out onto the dance floor. I shove myself close to him, then bury my face into his shoulder. I catch Sam's look of surprise as our gazes meet across the dance floor, and I turn my head away so that I'm looking at Kevin's neck. Wow. He actually has a very nice neck. Very smooth. And he smells really good too. Which is probably why I liked him in the first place. Although I don't remember noticing his neck before.

This is actually kind of nice, now that I'm getting into it. Just kind of swaying to the music, enjoying the feel of a boy's arms around me, melting into him. I just need to learn how to relax. But then, just as I'm about to, all of a sudden, Sam and Blake come waltzing into my view! He's danced her right around so that he can see me! Like it's not enough that he's dancing with my sister (wow, that sounds weird), now he's rubbing it in my face!

I squeeze my eyes shut, but it's too tempting. I can't look away. I watch them for a few seconds, the way he holds her close, and before I can stop myself, before I even know what's happening, I'm running off the dance floor and into the hall that leads to the bridal suite where my mom was getting ready.

It takes me a second to realize that Kevin followed me.

"Sorry," I say, swallowing the tears that are this close to spilling down my cheeks. "I just . . . I wanted to be alone for a second."

He nods, like he understands, which I should have figured he would. I mean, he's so nice. He's probably going to go out there and, like, sit at our table by himself now and start talking to my aunt Gertrude, who's, like, the most boring person in the world. She writes children's books (totally unpublished), and is always telling you about them or asking for your opinion on them. He probably realizes that I need my privacy and my space, and he's willing to give it to me because he's so nice and understanding.

"I understand," Kevin says. (See?) "I wanted to be alone too. I've wanted to be alone since the second we got here."

What? What is he talking about? He's wanted to be alone since the second he got here? Does that mean he's wanted to ditch me this whole time? Talk about adding insult to injury. Now not only does the boy I actually like want to ditch me, but the boy I don't even like at all wants to ditch me too!

But then I realize Kevin is getting . . . um, kind of close to me. Kind of close as in, um, invading-my-personal-space kind of close. Invading-my-personal-lip-space kind of close, if you want to get really specific.

And then, before I know it, he's leaning in and kissing me. His lips are on mine. It's not a bad kiss, actually. It's just . . . not like kissing Sam. And when I pull away, I look over Kevin's shoulder. And there's Sam, standing there, watching the whole thing.

sixteen

I'VE KISSED TWO BOYS. IN THE SPAN OF, like, two weeks I've kissed two boys. Actually, that's not true. Two boys have kissed me. I went from having no boys kissing me to two boys kissing me. I had no idea I was so kissable. It's very weird. But maybe it's like the law of averages or something, where if the average thirteen-year-old girl has kissed two boys in her lifetime, and I'd kissed zero, eventually it all had to even out. And it just happened to do that pretty quickly.

"I cannot believe our parents are going away for two whole weeks," Blake says the next day. We're both still curled up in our beds, trying to recover from the wedding yesterday. After Sam saw me kissing Kevin (or Kevin kissing me? I guess both, since I did kind of kiss him back—but only because I was caught off guard and my mouth just kind of, like, started kissing him back), he turned around and just left.

The rest of the wedding passed by without any more incidents, and actually, it's all kind of a blur now.

"Can *you?*" Blake presses. She's still snuggled up under the covers, with this perfectly content look on her face, which is, like, the exact opposite of how I'm feeling inside.

"Can I what?"

"Can you believe that our parents are leaving us alone for a whole week?"

"We're not going to be alone," I say. "Your brother is going to be here." At first my mom and Will wanted to hire, like, a nanny or something, but Blake and I pitched a fit, and so they finally relented and said that since it was going to be midterm time for Blake's brother, Randy, he could come and stay with us. They're paying him, like, four hundred dollars or something, which I think is a bit extreme. I mean, he's not even going to be doing that much. We're thirteen! We can pretty much take care of ourselves. But with the kind of money Randy's getting, I figure he should at least be good for walking Gus once in a while. I look down to the end of the bed warily, where Gus is sitting, staring up at me.

"It'll be pretty much be like we're alone," she says. "Seriously, Randy isn't going to care what we do. Maybe we should have another party! Or we could have Sam and Kevin over, that would be fun!"

Oh, yeah, that would be a real blast. "Maybe," I say.

Do. Not. Want. To. Get. Out. Of. Bed.

If Sunday doesn't start, then Monday won't ever come, and then I won't have to tell Ms. Tosh that I'm the one who used the manual override. I also won't have to see Kevin or Sam. The only bright spot in this whole thing is that Sam didn't kiss Blake at the wedding. Blake thinks it's because he was too shy. But that doesn't make sense because he kissed me, no problem. Unless he just likes her more, and I was just like, a kiss he didn't care about, so it was easy. Like how sometimes you can just work on something you don't even care about, and then it turns out amazing, and the projects you get really nervous about, you end up screwing up because they're so important.

Anyway, Sunday, of course, flies by in what seems like two seconds, and school's barely even started on Monday morning when I run into Ms. Tosh.

"Hello, Avery," Ms. Tosh says. She's standing by my locker, and she doesn't seem happy. Her face looks very dark and stern, like she's been waiting for this moment all weekend. Which she probably has. In fact, I'm surprised she didn't call my cell phone. She has the number on the student council contact sheet.

"Oh, hi," I say, pulling my stuff out of my locker slowly.

"I need to talk to you."

"I need to talk to you, too," I say. "But, um, do you think we could maybe do it after lunch? I have to stop by Mr. Bright's room and ask him a question about my social studies project." Now that the moment's here, I want to put it off as long as I can.

"It's really important," she says. "Did you know I was looking for you on Friday?" Oh, God. Now she's going to bring up the fact that I blew off all her pages. Which isn't good. And then it hits me. A completely brilliant plan! Deny that I had anything to do with it, and then tell her that I am resigning from student council due to the fact that I have too many other commitments!

Which isn't really true, since right now I have no other commitments. Why don't I have any other commitments? That's definitely not the way to get into a good college, especially since I'm about to get kicked off student council. Note to self: Set up new extracurricular commitments.

Anyway, I can tell Sophie that I resigned from student council, which everyone knows pretty much means kicked out. I can just tell her I told the truth, and that Ms. Tosh didn't want to embarrass me, so she gave me the chance to resign. Sophie will spread it around, of course, that I mixed up the matches, so people won't think that she really got hooked up with Taylor Meachum. And most people will probably believe her, which should be good enough for her. Of course, I'll still have to tell Blake about kissing Sam, since there's still a chance Sophie might tell her. But maybe this will buy me some time. A few more days, at least, until Blake and Sam get really close, and he kisses her, too.

"Avery?" Ms. Tosh is asking. She's looking at me worriedly.

"Um, yes," I say. "Okay, fine, I can meet now."

I follow her down the stairs and up the hall.

"So listen," I say as we're walking into the classroom. I want to make sure I cut her off at the pass, but then I realize "So listen" probably isn't the most respectful way to start off. Of course, manipulating the matches is where I lost all my respectfulness, so at this point starting a conversation with "So listen" probably isn't that big of a deal. Still, I decide to start over. "Thank you for calling this meeting," I try. I sit down in one of the front rows of chairs in her classroom. "It's very important that we talk."

"Yes," she says, before I can tell her that I'm resigning. "We need to talk about who's going to replace Sam as your unofficial second in command. I think Rina is the obvious choice, don't you?"

I frown and look at her. "Replace—what are you talking about?" Is it possible that I've misheard her? That maybe I've gone so crazy that I don't even know what people are saying anymore?

"We have a lot more projects coming up," she says. "The ski trip, for example. And since Sam has been so involved in everything you've been doing, I'm wondering who can step up and take his place."

"But why?" I ask, still confused.

"He didn't talk to you?"

"Um, no," I say.

"He told me he was going to tell you himself," she says. "But I guess he didn't." Ms. Tosh sighs, then leans back in her chair and puts her fingers on her temples. "Sam was the one who fixed the results," she says. "He was the one who fixed the matches."

"No, he wasn't," I blurt, and my mouth drops open.

"I know it's hard to believe," Ms. Tosh says, "since Sam has always been so conscientious in the past. But he came to me on Thursday and told me he was responsible. That's why I was trying to find you, so I could let you know and we could brainstorm some solutions to the problems his absence is going to cause."

My head is spinning around and around and around, and suddenly I can't breathe. He took the blame. He took the blame for me. And then on Saturday, he saw me at the wedding with Kevin, he saw me *kissing* Kevin. I can't even imagine how that must have made him feel.

I take a deep breath and turn to Ms. Tosh. "Ms. Tosh," I say, squaring my shoulders and looking her right in the eye, "Sam wasn't the one who fixed the matches. I was."

She didn't freak out. Ms. Tosh, I mean. She didn't scream or yell or tell me I was off student council. Of course, that's because she didn't know who to believe. She doesn't know if it's me or Sam who's telling the truth. I think she was leaning toward thinking that maybe we both had something to do with it, but she just sent me on my way and told me she would talk to our principal, Mr. Standish, to set up a meeting, and then get back to me on how things were going to proceed.

As soon as I got out of her classroom, I started texting Sam. Then I texted Sophie and told her that I'd confessed. I figured at this point, the whole resignation thing was stupid. The jig was up. Now I just have to hope that she doesn't tell Blake until I get a chance to talk to her. I texted Blake too, right after homeroom, and asked her if we could spent some time together after school, that I had to talk to her about something really important. But by the time lunch rolls around, none of them have texted me back. So when I get to the caf, I'm kind of freaking out. Rina and Jess are just sitting there, eating their sandwiches like nothing is going on, and I feel like I'm going to lose my mind.

"What's with you?" Rina asks about halfway through lunch. "We've been trying to gossip with you about Sophie's party this weekend, but you seem like you're in a different world."

"No, I'm not," I say, rolling my eyes.

"Spill it," Rina says. "What's going on with you?"

"Yeah," Jess says. "Spill."

I start to shake my head, but then I stop. Why haven't I told them? As far as I know, they're good at keeping secrets. They wouldn't judge me. They'd probably be really sympathetic. But I can't. Yes, they're my friends, and yes, they're really nice, but I can't take the chance of Blake finding out about me and Sam until I tell her myself this afternoon.

"I'm fine," I say. "I'm just not feeling that great. Bad stomach." It's not even a lie. I'm wrapping my sandwich back up and putting it in my bag when Blake comes over to the table. She slams her tray down, and the silverware next to her salad bowl goes bouncing off and onto the floor.

"Wow," Rina says. "What's with you guys today?"

"Yeah," Jess says. "You're both being really weird."

"You should ask Avery," Blake says, her eyes flashing. "I'm sure she'd be happy to tell you what's going on."

"What do you mean?" I ask. But it comes out hardly above a whisper. Because I know. I know what she's going to say next. I knew, deep in my heart, that Sophie couldn't be trusted. I knew I should have told Blake before this. I knew, I knew, I knew.

"You know what I mean," she says. "About how you kissed Sam."

I gasp. Rina gasps. Jess gasps. Even Blake gasps, and she's the one who said it.

"Blake, I—"

"Save it," she says, and then gets up and waltzes over to Sophie Burns's table. She flips her hair behind her ears, and then Sophie reaches over and gives Blake a half hug, all while shooting me daggers with her eyes.

Rina and Jess are staring at me, their eyes bugging out of their heads.

"I'm sorry I didn't tell you," I say. "I just—I didn't—" My eyes start to fill with tears, and I quickly shove the rest of my lunch into my bag and run out of the cafeteria. No one follows me.

seventeen

THE REST OF THE DAY PASSES IN A BLUR,
and when the final bell rings, the idea of going home
and facing Blake is too much to bear. How can we be
in the same house, in the same *room* even (whose crazy
idea was that to let us share a room even temporarily?
I mean, how stupid, we're two teenage girls, there definitely was going to be some kind of drama) after what
happened? Instead, I decide to stay after and work on
some homework in the library. But I can't concentrate,
and I keep checking my phone to see if Sam texted me
back (he hasn't).

Finally, when it's almost time for the late buses to
line up, I decide to swing by the gym and catch him
on his way out of lacrosse practice. I don't even know
what I want to say to him. I just know that I have to talk

to him, that I have to ask him why he tried to take the blame for what I did. I have to ask him if he likes me, if he likes Blake, and how I'm supposed to deal with all of this.

I lean against the wall outside of the gym, feeling embarrassed and out of place as all the guys come trailing out of the locker room.

"Avery!" I hear my name and turn around. Oh. Kevin.

"Hi, Kevin," I say, trying to figure out how to get rid of him without being rude. He's been texting me ever since the wedding on Saturday, but I haven't texted him back, mostly because I just didn't really know what to say to him.

"Hey," he says. "You haven't replied to any of my texts."

"I know," I say. "I'm sorry, I just . . . I had a really busy rest of the weekend."

"I understand." He shifts his weight back and forth on his sneakers and smiles at me shyly. "So I had a really good time with you at the wedding."

"I had a nice time too," I lie. And then, over Kevin's shoulder, I see Sam finally coming out of the locker room. My eyes lock onto his, and then he looks away and pushes past us and out the door.

"Listen, Kevin," I say. "I'm sorry, I just . . . I only like you as a friend." It's kind of weird to be so blunt, but I can't waste any more time. I need to get to Sam before he gets on his bus.

"A friend?" Kevin looks startled. "Really? Do you always kiss your friends like that?"

"No," I say. "The truth is, I—I like someone else. I'm sorry, I'll text you later."

And then I'm rushing down the hall after Sam.

"Hey!" I yell when I finally reach him. But he keeps walking, and for a second, I think maybe he hasn't heard me, but when he quickens his pace, I realize he's just ignoring me. And walking really fast to get away from me. I run to catch up.

"Hey!" I say again. "Sam!" A couple of guys on his team turn from where they're standing on the sidewalk waiting for the buses and stare at me.

One of them says, "Oooh, Sam, I think she really wants to talk to you." Ugh. As if my life isn't a big enough mess, now I have to deal with jerky eighth-grade boys who think they're the funniest things ever.

"Hey!" I say to him, running up and blocking his path. "You can talk to me now, or I can make an even bigger scene."

He stops. Wow. I didn't know I had that in me. Although it's a good thing he stopped. Because honestly, that was kind of a lie. I wouldn't have made a bigger scene. Yelling his name was pretty much the biggest kind of scene I know how to make. And even if I *did* know how to make a bigger scene, I'm not so sure I'd be willing to do it. I mean, yeah, he's the potential love of my life, but even I know where to draw the line.

He sighs, then says, *"Fine,"* in this really low, annoyed voice that leads me to believe that this is going to be a short conversation. I follow him around the corner of the building, out of sight of everyone else, I guess because he's afraid I might freak out on him in front of his friends.

"What?" he says. He tightens his grip on the strap of his backpack and looks at me impatiently.

"I . . . um . . . I just wanted to say that I know you told Ms. Tosh you were the one who switched the matches." I look down at the ground. Suddenly, now that he's here in front of me, I don't know what to say, what I'm even doing here, why it was so important that I talk to him.

"Yeah?"

"And I wanted to say thanks." I pull my eyes up to his, and I can see how hurt he is. "And that I told her it was me."

"Trust me, you don't have to thank me," he says. "And if I'd known you liked Kevin, I wouldn't have done it."

"But why *did* you do it?" I ask.

"I did it because you love student council, and you deserve to be able to keep participating. The only reason you mixed up the matches was because you wanted to do something nice for Blake, and I really didn't think you should be punished for that."

"Well, that was really nice of you." I take a deep breath. "But like I said, I told Ms. Tosh the truth. And there's nothing going on between Kevin and me. I told him I just want to be friends." He doesn't say anything, just shifts his gym bag to his other shoulder and sighs, waiting for me to finish. "Um, because I, uh, I like someone else."

He looks at me, then raises his eyebrows, getting it. "Does Blake know?"

"That I like you? Yes," I say truthfully.

"You told her?"

"Sophie told her."

"That's what I thought." And then he turns around and walks toward the bus.

Ms. Tosh schedules a meeting for a week from now, for me, Sam, and our principal, Mr. Standish. The week drags and drags. Finally the day comes, and I dress for school. Blake isn't talking to me. She hasn't been talking to me all week. She's been talking to Sophie, though.

Every single day, they've been sitting together at lunch. And every single day, she's been freezing me out.

It's easy to keep up appearances at home, since Randy doesn't know what we're normally like, if we talk at all. He just chalks it up to normal stepsister stuff. Actually, I'm not even sure if he knows we're not talking, since he's not around that much. It's kind of ironic, actually, that once me and Blake became stepsisters, we immediately started fighting. I mean, how cliché.

The meeting is on an Indian summer day, one of those mornings that make you wonder if it's even fall. I reach deep into my closet and pull out a bright summer dress, one of the things that Blake and I bought when we went to the mall on our sisters day.

I'm hoping the bright colors of the dress will cheer me up, but they don't.

I head down to Mr. Standish's office as soon as I get to school, glad that they're not calling me down over the loudspeaker. That would just add to the humiliation. When I get there, Sam's already there, sitting in one of the folding chairs outside the office. When Mr. Standish calls us in, Ms. Tosh is in the office, in a chair on the side of his desk, and Sam and I sit down across from them.

"Now," Mr. Standish says. "It's come to my attention that there's been some tomfoolery going on with the student council project." Leave it to Mr. Standish to use a word like "tomfoolery." Mr. Standish is very old, and he uses words that are completely out of date and old-fashioned. He has kind eyes and white hair, and he likes to wear bow ties, but he's still very scary since he's the principal. "And it seems as if you're both attempting to take responsibility for it. Is that true?"

I take a deep breath, look at Mr. Standish, and say, "Sir, I'd like to put this matter to rest right now."

He looks up at me, then leans back in his chair and crosses his hands on his desk. "Oh?"

"Yes," I say. "I'm the one who's responsible for this. Sam had nothing to do with it."

"Sam says he did," Mr. Standish says. Sam doesn't say anything. He doesn't deny it or try to stop me. He doesn't say that he's the one who did it after all. But it wouldn't matter if he did. Whether or not he wants to take the blame doesn't matter anymore.

"But he didn't," I say. "I did. And I can prove it."

"How?" Ms. Tosh asks.

"Ask Sam who Blake got matched up with," I say. "I changed her match too. Ask him."

As far as I know, Blake hasn't told Sam who her match was. Why would she tell the guy she likes that she got matched up with someone else?

Ms. Tosh looks down at her paper. "It's true," she says. "The manual override was used on Blake's match." She turns to Sam. "Sam? Do you know who Blake got matched up with?"

"Um . . ." For a second, he looks like maybe he's going to take a guess at it. But finally he sighs and says, "No, I don't."

"Avery?" Ms. Tosh says.

"It was Kevin Hudson," I say. "Kevin Hudson is the one I matched Blake up with."

I stare down at my shoes. Ms. Tosh looks down at the incident report, then turns to Mr. Standish and nods.

"Okay," Mr. Standish says. "Sam, you may go back to class. Avery, please stay here so that we can decide what to do."

eighteen

THEY DON'T KICK ME OUT. THEY COULD. But they don't, because of my "exemplary past record." But they're not going to let me run for any student council offices next year, and they're taking me off the record as the person who ran the charity project. Which I guess means I won't be able to use it on my college applications, but honestly, who even cares about that right now? The boy I love isn't speaking to me, my new stepsister isn't speaking to me, and Ms. Tosh said that once our parents get back from their honeymoon, she's going to have to call them and tell them what happened. Which means *they* won't be speaking to me.

I'm in such a bad mood that when I get home, I go right upstairs and into my room. There's a package sitting on my bed, and I open it. It's charms. Charms that

I ordered off the internet as the perfect late birthday present for Blake. One for me and one for her. For our sisters bracelets. They're small, gold, like a name necklace almost, but with the word "sister" written in swirly calligraphy letters.

But now I can't give it to her. Now everything is ruined. I put the charms under my pillow and bury my face into the pillowcase, letting the sobs come pouring out. After a few minutes, I feel something cold and wet under my hand. Gus. I open my eyes, and he looks at me with concern.

"It's okay, boy," I tell him. "I'm just sad."

He jumps up on the bed, licks my check, and then lays his head on my pillow. And that's how we fall asleep.

I sleep for the rest of the afternoon and all through the night, then wake up to the sound of dishes being stacked downstairs. When I get to the kitchen, Blake's sitting at the table, eating some pasta.

"Angeline sent it over," she says.

"Oh." I make myself a plate from the refrigerator, then sit down next to her. It's kind of weird to be having pasta for breakfast, but I'm not going to say anything, because it's delicious.

We eat the rest of the meal in silence, and then head

upstairs, where we take turns in the bathroom. When we get on the bus, I sit down in my usual seat in the middle, and Blake goes to the back.

The day passes at a snail's pace. Rina and Jess know something's up, but I don't tell them, and they don't press. I stay after school to work on my homework in the library again, mostly because I just don't feel like going home. On the late bus ride home, my mom texts me to ask how things are going, and I tell her they're fine and even add a big smiley face.

When I get off the bus, there's a truck in my driveway. At first I think it's probably one of Randy's friends—my parents told him under no circumstances was he allowed to have people over, but I'm assuming it's just a matter of time before he breaks that rule—but as I get closer, I see the big ANIMAL CONTROL lettering on the side.

Uh-oh. I pick up my pace and see Blake standing at the front door, talking to a man in a brown uniform with a mustache. Gus is frolicking at his feet, on the end of a long leash.

"I don't know why he would have run away like that," Blake's saying, using the same voice I usually do with grown-ups. "He's usually so calm and well-behaved." As she says this, Gus spots me and tries to jump off the steps and onto my legs. He starts whining and pulling at the leash.

"Is there a problem here?" I ask, mostly because that's what I've heard my mom say to people when she doesn't want to be messed with.

"Who are you?" the man says, looking down at me like I'm a bug.

"I'm Avery LaDuke," I say. "And who are you?"

"I'm Officer Grimshaw," he says. "The animal control officer who is in charge of this area."

"Nice to meet you," I say. "What can I do for you?"

"Officer Grimshaw was just bringing Gus back to us," Blake says. "I was telling him I had no idea how he could have gotten out, he's usually so very well-behaved."

"Very well-behaved," I say, nodding as Gus starts chewing on the leash that the officer is holding.

"Where are your parents?" Officer Grimshaw asks.

"They're away on their honeymoon," I say. "They won't be back until Monday."

"Who's in charge of you girls?" Officer Grimshaw wants to know. Seriously, he's kind of overstepping his bounds, if you ask me. It's not really his business who's in charge of us.

"Our older brother is taking care of us," Blake says.

"But he's taking a midterm right now. He's in college. Harvard."

It's not true, of course. Randy goes to Framingham State, and from what I've heard, he was lucky to get in there.

"He's not even my real brother," I say. "Our parents just got married, so he's my stepbrother."

Blake, getting what I'm going for, gives a sad sniff. "Yes," she says. "It's been a rough transition for all of us, especially with Granny passing away. That's probably why Gus here is acting so strange. He can sense the tension in the house."

"Dogs are very attuned emotionally," Officer Grimshaw says, nodding. He looks down at Gus. "Well, he doesn't seem dangerous, just a little high-strung, and you showed me the paper that says he has all his shots." He hands it back to Blake. "I'll let you guys go with a warning this time, but if I get called back here . . ." He trails off, like we're going to be in big, big trouble.

"It won't happen again, Officer," I say.

"We promise," Blake chimes in.

Officer Grimshaw nods, and gets back into his truck.

"Thanks," I say to Blake shyly.

"You're welcome."

We walk into the house, and I shut the door. "I wonder

how he got out," I say. I head out to the backyard, and Blake follows me. We find a gap in the wooden fence, where a piece of wood has rotted out. We build up a huge stone wall in front of it, using a bunch of rocks from the backyard.

"There," I say. "That will keep him in."

Gus, obviously not realizing that he's being confined, dances and jumps around the backyard happily.

And that's when I see it. The sister charm. On Blake's bracelet.

"Where did you get that?" I blurt.

"Oh," she says, fingering the tiny piece of jewelry. "It was on your desk. There were . . . there were two of them, so I figured one must be for me. Sorry, I didn't mean to—"

"No, it's fine," I say. "One *was* for you, for your birthday, I just didn't . . . I didn't think you'd want to wear it."

She's still looking at the charm, running her fingers over the connecting letters, and then she finally looks up at me. "Is it true that you fixed the student council project so that I could get hooked up with Sam?"

"Who told you that?" I ask.

"Sam." I don't say anything for a second. "So did you?" she presses.

"Yes," I say finally, because she's going to find out sooner or later. I mean, Ms. Tosh is going to call my parents and then she'll definitely wonder why I'm being grounded/disowned/insert horrible punishment here.

"That was really nice of you," she says. "Since I know you like him."

"I didn't," I lie. "I mean, I don't."

"Avery," she says, grinning, "you like him. It's obvious. I kind of started figuring it out at the wedding."

"You did?"

"Yeah." She sighs, and a breeze comes floating by and ruffles her hair. "And he likes you, too. He told me."

"He *did* like me," I say. "But he doesn't anymore."

"You could fix it," she says.

I shake my head. "No way," I say. "You like him."

She rolls her eyes. "I did like him," she says. "But not the way you like him. I liked him because he was cute and popular, not because we actually have anything in common."

"Really?"

"Yeah," she says. "And besides, I think I kind of like Brayden Stone."

"Brayden's nice," I say. I take a deep breath, crossing my fingers. "So are we cool?"

"Yeah," she says, grinning. "But one more thing. Why

didn't you tell me about you and Sophie?"

"What about me and Sophie?"

"About how you guys used to be friends? And how she told you that she would tell me you kissed Sam unless you told Ms. Tosh you fixed the matchmaking results?"

"She told you that?"

"Yeah," Blake says. "She was, like, bragging about it."

"Ugh," I say.

"Yeah, ugh," she says. "Why didn't you tell me how horrible she was?"

"I don't know," I say. "I guess I didn't want you to think I was being jealous. Or that I was a loser because she didn't like me."

"I wouldn't have thought that," she says. "We're sisters. Sisters trump mean girls anytime."

I smile at her. She smiles at me. And once we're inside, I head upstairs and fasten my own sister charm to my bracelet.

Randy has a late class until nine o'clock, so Blake and I decide to turn the family room into a movie theater. We set up the couches in a row, close all the blinds, dim the lights, pop popcorn and drizzle it with butter, and then set up bowls full of candy on the coffee table.

We're just about to put the movie in when suddenly I

realize I haven't heard Gus barking in the backyard for at least ten minutes. And ten minutes without barking in Gus time is like a lifetime.

"We should bring the dogs in here," I say. I go to the back door, and Princess bounds up over the deck and through the sliding glass door, but I can't see Gus anywhere.

"Blake!" I yell. "I can't find Gus!"

"What?" she says, coming up the stairs and to the door. "What do you mean you can't find him?"

"I mean he was in the backyard and now he's not there anymore." I'm shoving my feet into my sneakers and snagging my coat off the coatrack. Blake does the same, and we run out into the yard.

We see the hole pretty much right away. A huge hole dug under the fence. "He's gone," I say, as Blake runs up to me. "He dug a hole and he's gone."

Blake goes down one side of the street, and I go down the other. Why, why, why did I let him out into the backyard? Now he's going to get caught by Officer Grimshaw, and who knows what he'll do to him! Take him away from us, put him back in that awful shelter?

"Gus! Gus! Gus!" I'm screaming as I walk all around the block, looking for him.

I'm halfway up the other side of the street when I hear the footsteps. I turn around to see Sam walking behind me, his hands shoved into the pockets of his coat. He catches up to me and hands me his hat wordlessly.

I'm about to protest, but I was in such a rush to get out that I forgot my own hat, and my ears are freezing. "Thanks," I say, putting it on.

"How'd he get out?"

"Dug a hole under the fence," I say. "And—and—I should have been watching him and now . . ." I start to cry.

"Hey, hey, it's okay," he says. "We'll find him, he's probably just running around."

He reaches over and takes my hand, and squeezes it. And he doesn't let go.

Fifteen minutes later we're still looking. We've been up and down every street on this side of the neighborhood, and Blake, who's been texting me with updates, has been up and down every street on the other side of the neighborhood.

It's only when we're circling back around toward Sam's grandma's house that we see him. He's sitting on the front porch, looking at us like he doesn't know what the big fuss is about.

"Gus!" I scream, running up the stairs and onto the porch.

"I guess he wanted to visit," Sam says as Gus jumps up and licks my face. I'm so relieved to have him back that I can't even be mad at him. I'm just so glad he's okay.

"Thanks for helping me try to find him," I say, as Gus's tail wags happily and he shimmies and shakes all over the porch.

"No problem."

I stand up. "Um, well," I say. "I guess I should go home now."

"Yeah," he says.

"Thanks for telling Blake," I blurt. "About the project. About what I did."

"It was important," he says. "I know how much she means to you. She needed to know you were looking out for her. Are you guys friends again?"

"Yeah," I say. "We're totally fine." I swallow. "Are we?"

"Friends again?"

"No," I say. "Are we . . . I mean . . ." I take another deep breath. "I told Blake I like you."

"You did?"

"Well, she already knew," I say. "Because of Sophie. And I'm sorry she had to hear it from Sophie, I really am. I just . . . I didn't know what to do. I didn't want to hurt anyone, you know?"

He hesitates, but then he nods. "Yeah," he says. "I get it. It must have been really hard for you."

"It was," I say.

"So does this mean she's okay with it?"

"With what?"

"With me and you?"

"Like, me and you together?"

"Yeah," he says, smiling and taking a step toward me. "Me and you. Together."

"Yes," I say. He's closer now, and then his lips are on mine, and I melt into him, not thinking about anything but the kiss. My parents are going to be home next week, and they're going to find out what I did, and they're going to be mad, and I'm going to have to figure out a way to keep Gus in the backyard, and what kind of extracurricular activity I want to get into to replace student council, and how I'm going to deal with Sophie, but for now, there's just this. Me and Sam. And Blake, waiting for me at home.

"Can I walk you home now?" he asks.

"Yes," I say.

And so he does.

Girl Meets Ghost

You know how sometimes you're doing something totally important, like picking out the perfect Stila lip gloss, or staring at the back of Brandon Dunham's neck during math (trust me, he has a very cute neck), and you get interrupted by something horribly annoying, like an unwanted text message or a teacher calling on you? Yeah, welcome to my world. Only, a lot of the time it's not my phone or a teacher interrupting me. A lot of the time it's a ghost. I see them. I listen to them. And then I do whatever they tell me so that they can get closure and move on to wherever it is ghosts go.

Like right now, for example. I'm in math, and this girl ghost (usually the ghosts are girls—I'm not sure why that is, and it's not like I can ask someone what the rules are) just shows up, dressed like a gymnast, and starts doing cartwheels and flips! Right down the aisle between the rows of desks!

Of course she's blond (figures), around sixteen (figures), and really beautiful (figures, figures, figures). She's all, "Kendall, help me!"

And my dad wonders why my math grades are so bad. It's because of distractions like this (and Brandon Dunham's neck, which, as previously mentioned, is very, very nice).

"Kendall Williams?" my math teacher, Mr. Jacobi, says from the front of the room.

"I'm sorry," I say in my most polite tone. "Can you repeat the number of the problem you'd like answered?"

"I don't want a problem answered," Mr. Jacobi says. "I want you to tell me what you got on your quiz, so that I can record it in my grade book."

"Oh," I say. "Um, seventy-two."

Mr. Jacobi gives me a little bit of a disgusted look, like, *Wow, if I'd gotten that grade, I wouldn't want it recorded either,* and then moves on. Mr. Jacobi is definitely not my biggest fan. It's mostly because I just cannot seem to get a handle on the quadratic formula. And that isn't even really my fault. My dad said that the quadratic formula is super-hard, and he never learned it until ninth grade. And I'm only in seventh. Which seems really unfair. They're just moving formulas up, like, two whole grade levels.

The bell rings then, and I sigh and gather up my new math binder. I bought it last night in an effort to get myself more interested in math. It's this sparkly aqua color, and it has a place to put pics of you and all your friends on the inside. Of course, I haven't gotten around to that part yet.

I glance out of the corner of my eye at Little Miss Gymnast. She's sitting over on the windowsill now, stretching out her legs. I wonder why she's still doing that when she's obviously dead. I mean, once you're a ghost, you really don't have to worry about your body anymore. But since she's a beautiful teenager, she probably won't believe me when I tell her that. Sigh.

At least she knows she's dead. That's one of the good things about seeing ghosts. I don't ever have to tell them they're dead. They already know, which is good, because can you imagine? It would be super-horrible if I had to tell them.

I let out another big sigh, and it must be a lot louder than I thought, because Brandon Dunham turns around and says, "I wouldn't worry about it, Kendall. It's just a quiz. You can make it up."

I guess he thinks I'm upset about my grade. Brandon Dunham knows all about my math grades. Mr. Jacobi makes us pass our quizzes to the person in front of us to grade, and Brandon sits in front of me. Which is really not fair. To make it even worse, then Mr. Jacobi goes around the room and you have to say your grade out loud so that he can record it. So the whole class knows how bad you did, which is *really* not fair.

"Yeah," I say. "I'm sure I can make it up." Sometimes Brandon and I talk. You know, just about little things, like we're doing now. I've been trying to work out how I can push us into we're-friends-and-talk-about-other-things-besides-school territory, but, like the quadratic formula, I haven't quite figured that out yet.

"You can," Brandon says. "I know once you get the hang of this stuff, you'll be able to do it in no time."

Hmmph. Easy for him to say. Brandon is, like, a math genius or something. He always gets 98 on his quizzes. I know this because of the whole saying-our-grades-out-loud thing.

And then I have it. The most perfect, brilliant idea ever.

"I don't know," I say, looking down at my binder and hoping I sound forlorn. "It's getting a little late in the year for me to be able to catch up."

Brandon looks confused. "It's only October."

"Yeah, well, it's never too early to start thinking about your future." This is a very smart thing to say. My dad always says it, and he's pretty much the smartest person I know. Of course, whenever *he* says it, I always just blow it off, because who really listens when their parents say something like that? But I can still appreciate the smartness of it.

"I guess." Brandon turns around to leave, and I see him slipping out of my grasp, like a slippery little fish.

"I wish," I say really loud and pointedly, "that I had someone to tutor me."

"They have an after-school tutoring program," Brandon says. "They meet every Wednesday after school. It's down in the math lab."

"Thanks," I say. "I'll definitely look into that. But it's too bad that we have another quiz tomorrow. You know, before I'll have a chance to get to the math lab."

"We have another quiz tomorrow?" Brandon starts leafing through his planner. It's a lie, of course. We don't have another quiz tomorrow, but can't the guy get the hint that I want him to tutor me? I mean, seriously. My dad says I'm about as subtle as a Mack truck. So either Brandon is really dense or I'm not doing a good job of getting my point across.

"Well, no," I say, because I realize that if he thinks we're going to have a quiz and we don't, he'll know I lied. "I just have a lot of anxiety about quizzes, so I tell myself that we have them every day. You know, so I'll make sure to study." Brandon nods, like this makes perfect sense to him. "Plus I'm going to ask Mr. Jacobi if I can do a makeup quiz tomorrow. To erase my grade. But only if I can study a lot tonight."

This whole time the blond gymnast in the corner has been watching with fascination. She probably thinks I'm crazy. I bet she always had, like, three bazillion boys asking her out all the time, and used to date the hottest guy in school. But I don't care if she's watching. Ghosts don't really make me self-conscious. I mean, how can they? They're dead. No matter how amazing they used to be, I still have one thing over them: I'm alive.

"You can do it," Brandon says. He shoots me his amazing smile. He has the most amazing perfectly straight white teeth. And his eyes twinkle. Seriously. His eyes twinkle when he smiles. Like a prince in a Disney cartoon or something.

He turns to go, and I sigh yet again.

"Oh, for God's sake," Blond Gymnast says, vaulting off the windowsill in one smooth movement. "If you want to study with him, then just ASK HIM." I cock my head and give her an incredulous look. "Do it!" she says. I give her an even more incredulous look. "Boys are dumb," she says. "He doesn't get it."

He doesn't? That seems a little unlikely, since I was practically throwing myself at him. But I guess she could be right. I definitely buy into the whole boys-are-dumb thing, and this girl seems like the kind of person who would know about stuff like this.

"Hey!" I yell at Brandon's back, right as he's about to walk out of the classroom. "Do you want to study together? Today? After school? In the library?" Blond Gymnast rolls her eyes, I guess because she knows that I'm making a big mess out of asking him. But what does she want from me? It's a miracle I even asked him in the first place.

"Sure," Brandon says. "I'll meet you after eighth. Is it okay if Kyle comes?"

"Of course," I say, my heart soaring.

"Finally!" Blond Gymnast says, once Brandon's out the door of the classroom. "Now we can get to my problem. Which is way worse than some middle school study date." Right. There's that. And figuring out who Kyle is.

I've been able to see ghosts pretty much as long as I can remember. My mom left me and my dad when I was just a few months old, and so at first my dad thought I was making up all these imaginary friends because I was looking for a mother figure.

He thought I'd grow out of it, but I didn't, and right around the time I turned eight, I figured it probably wasn't the best idea to bring it up anymore. My dad was totally overwhelmed with everything he had going on—raising a daughter all by himself, keeping up our house, and working super-long hours trying to get his contracting business off the ground. So I decided it was best to stop talking about it, since he was starting to act all worried every time I brought it up. I realized it was pretty abnormal to see ghosts, and so I haven't told anyone since.

I'm not sure exactly when I figured out that if I help the ghosts, they leave. It's kind of like asking someone when they realized that they loved their parents, or that they liked chocolate. It was just . . . there. Obviously I couldn't help the ghosts when I was younger. I just saw them kind of milling about. They'd come and hang out with me when they were bored, or needed someone to talk at. It seemed like they enjoyed seeing me as a baby and as a little kid, I guess because it reminded them of the circle of life or whatever.

Anyway, I'm much older now—twelve, almost thirteen,

and in seventh grade—so obviously I'm in a much better position to help people. Although you'd be surprised at how many ghosts get annoyed when they realize I'm the one who's going to give them what they need to move into the afterlife. They pitch fits about me being so young. Can you imagine? It's like, beggars can't be choosers, you know? And I'm really good at what I do. I've never met a ghost that I couldn't help.

Still, I try not to get too upset with them if they get cranky. They are dead, after all.

Anyway, it becomes pretty obvious that Blond Gymnast is going to be the kind of ghost that tries my patience, because as we head out of math, she starts to freak out.

"Hello!" she's shrieking as we walk down the hall to my next class. "Are you going to help me or what?"

Sometimes the best thing to do with ghosts is just ignore them until they realize that shouting and stuff won't get them anywhere. They also need to understand that I have to work with them on my own time. You know, when I'm alone and can talk to them without people thinking I'm crazy. Usually they get the message pretty quickly, but not this time. Blond Gymnast is pushy.

"I know you have *sooo* much to think about," she says, all snotty, "with your little study date and all, but this is important. Life-and-death stuff."

I seriously doubt that, because she's already dead. So it can't *really* be a matter of life and death. Unless she's talking metaphorically, which I guess she could be. Even though she probably doesn't even know the meaning of the word "metaphorical." I laugh to myself, but this makes Blond Gymnast angry. "Hello!" she shrieks again. "Over here, Lady Gaga!"

I gasp. I know exactly why she's calling me Lady Gaga. Lady Gaga is known for her crazy sense of fashion and hairstyles. And today I'm sporting my hair in a very cute style of three tiny braids to the side, then pushed back off my face and held with three tiny glitter clips. I like to do my hair to match my mood, and this morning I was feeling very whimsical. It's all I can do not to dignify this with a response, and I just keep marching to French class.

"Fine!" she says, throwing her hands up in the air. "For some reason you are pretending not to hear me." Um, maybe because if I talk to you, people will think I'm crazy? "I'll meet you after school. In the library."

Great. Looks like my date with Brandon is now going to be a double.

Sometimes a girl just needs a good book.
Lauren Barnholdt understands.

www.laurenbarnholdt.com

From Aladdin M!X   Published by Simon & Schuster

IF YOU ♥ THIS BOOK,
you'll love all the rest from

YOUR HOME AWAY FROM HOME:

AladdinMix.com

HERE YOU'LL GET:

- ♥ The first look at new releases
- ♥ Chapter excerpts from all the Aladdin M!X books
- ♥ Videos of your fave authors being interviewed

Did you **LOVE** this book?

Wan to get access to great books for **FREE?**

Join

Simon & Schuster **IN THE** **book loop**

<u>where you can</u>

✳ Read great books for FREE! ✳

⦂ Get exclusive excerpts ⦂

⧄ Chat with your friends ⧄

◉ Vote on polls ◎

Log on to ∞ everloop.com

and join the book loop group!

Rachel Renée Russell

DORK diaries

New York Times Bestselling Series

Have YOU read all of Nikki Maxwell's diaries?

MOST IMPORTANT TIP EVER FROM NIKKI MAXWELL:

Always let your inner DORK shine through!

Jammed full of surprises!

LiP SMACKER®
LOUNGE